amy evans

CLICKS

the DOLPHIN prophecy

book one

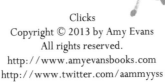

Clicks
Copyright © 2013 by Amy Evans
All rights reserved.
http://www.amyevansbooks.com
http://www.twitter.com/aammyyss

This is a work of fiction. Any resemblance of characters to actual persons,
living or dead, is purely coincidental.

Edition 1.6

Credits
Developmental Editor – Jennifer Rees
Copy Editor – Rhiannon Paille
Cover Design by Regina Wamba - Mae I Design
Formatting by Inkstain Interior Book Designing

what are clicks?

WAVES THAT EXPERIENCED surfers sense instinctively before they can be seen or heard. Winners trust their clicks and get in position, dropping in on the beginning swell and taking even the biggest monsters on a ride. Then there are the rest of us. We wait; jump on at the wrong time. Best case, we hang on. Worst, we're sent crashing to the ocean floor trying desperately not to drown.

The ocean never clicked for me. Not like it did for my brother, or my grandmother, or the many ancestors who'd come before. Still, they expected me to commit for life, guarding the ocean and the land, just because I was first born. I wanted none of it. But I let them train me so that I could win the Surf Carnival and get the heck out of town.

So I begged the universe for clicks, and when they came, fast, furious, I couldn't catch them fast enough. These waves weren't tricks to be tamed. They were warnings from the universe that everything would change. But I didn't listen with my heart or trust the messaging to stop the disasters before they came.

And even when I wasn't in the water, it felt like I had downed.

dedication

THE VERY FIRST copy is for Ginger, who inspired me to create a Utopyan world where girls learn to develop their intuition. To Rex, who taught me that even baby dinosaurs can swim like dolphins if they practice hard enough. To my dad, who showed me that making connections other people do not is a very special gift. To my mom, who's been there 1000% and proves every day that hard work and lots of love will get you anywhere you want to be. And to my husband, Evan, who makes our life better than anything I could ever imagine. He takes my dreams seriously, weaves them together with his own, and does everything he can to make them come true.

An extra special thank you to all our family and friends for the support and encouragement. And triple shots of gratitude to Allison Hamilton-Rohe and Jennifer Henderson for keeping me sane, helping me focus and moving this forward, especially last summer when I really needed the extra help.

AMY — xoox

one

CAN'T WE JUST skip to the party? Mica clicked, disturbing me with his intense impatience. His average emotional temperature always burned higher and dipped lower than mine. His feelings influenced us more frequently, but I wanted to enjoy tonight.

Stop. Breathe. This is happening. Look around and enjoy it, ok? I clicked back, attempting to do the same.

Two sets of twins—me and Mica, and Andrew and Darwen. Blake stood by Shayla, mismatched because neither of their twins were there. Around us stood relatives; the combined generations of The Guard who'd prepared us for this since we were born.

"Welcome to First Night," said Stoney. He was Blake's grandfather and their rumbly voices were so much alike. "Please close your eyes."

Following orders, I concentrated on the shadows and flashes in my mind and let my other senses capture the moment. Briny saltwater and honeysuckle hit my nose, the wind shivering with expectation.

"On this First Night, we rededicate ourselves to an ancient covenant symbolized by this pin which represents the balance in our world. You join those who've come before you and vow to protect the ocean from land, nature from man. You may now look."

As head lifeguard, Stoney had top authority on our Island and the run of this ritual. Silver flashed through his long fingers, the famous pin. I recognized it without ever seeing it before. Stoney placed it on a central stone.

The pin needed to stand at a right angle to the ocean, representing the pivotal balance between ocean and land, animal, and man. When it did, our Island, our people, and the ocean stayed healthy. When it tilted, disease and disaster would come.

I held my breath, wondering how it looked for us this year. The pin wavered for just a moment, then landed perpendicular to the horizon line. A celebratory cheer went up all around us, and the music started again.

A combination of beats, claps, clicks, and hums were something I'd heard since birth, but never in a ceremony like this. Rhythm and music were a big part of Pinhold life. Visitors joined our weekly drum circles on the beach, and stayed to listen to the wave organ built into the cliffs that played a series of gongs at high tide. Tonight, they stirred that feeling of connection and continuity that had always eluded me before.

To the untrained ear, the clicks and whistles probably sounded like nothing more than rhythmic nonsense playing along with the beat. In reality they were imitations of the sounds made by the dolphins that lived in our bay—we were inviting them to join us and witness our commitment to protect their home.

"We call you to pledge yourself as the guardians of the sea. Witnessed by the sacred swirl, do you pledge to protect the ocean from land and the animals from man?" Stoney asked. His voice pulsed in time with the pounding drumbeats.

"Yes," said six voices in unison, including mine.

"Now, it is time to answer in the language of the ancients." Stoney instructed, keeping his voice low. "When I touch you, repeat after me."

Stoney started with Mica. The strange sounds rolled from his tongue with ease. Instantly I heard the dolphins chattering over the kicked up breeze. My heart jumped along with their increased activity in the water. Legend said we needed them to witness our pledge, but they didn't come for every ritual anymore.

As each of my friends took the vow, the dolphins' talk faded, as if they headed the wrong way. The tension grew palpable until Blake spoke, when the noise got louder, but not closer. Finally, my turn came.

I inhaled deeply and shut my eyes, seeing the location of the dolphins clearly in my mind. They frolicked in the riptide off towards the open ocean. They heard us calling them but did not swim closer to watch. For maximum success, we needed them to join our swim. My heart churned as I realized now, that was all up to me.

I wondered how on earth I'd reach them with my low, scratchy voice. Speaking loudly never worked well for me. Then, I heard their noises change as they went under the surface to play and swim even further from us.

You can do this clicked Mica, straight into my brain. *Slow and low.* He said the syllables silently, emphasizing all the proper points for inflection. With this info, I realized Stoney hadn't repeated it perfectly. Somehow Mica had already learned which tones to pay attention to.

I repeated it silently then spoke it as loudly as possible. My voice lacked volume but I added energy by sending vibrations swirling through my bones, through the rocks and into the water, hoping to reach the dolphins below the surface.

They reacted instantly, repeating the clicks and whistles I made sound for sound. Quickly they moved towards me, churning through the thirty-foot sea waves that made Pinhold a famous surfing spot.

"Again!" Stoney said, insistently. I listened, repeating myself five more times, until the dolphins came right into the bay. The mood shifted and I opened my eyes to the pure joy of their arrival. As if sensing my attention, the huge pod began playing and showing off. They flipped, jumped and twisted in the air.

"Well done," Stoney said, looking proud of us all. "Now, go join the guardians of the sea for the traditional swim."

I took a second to appreciate their silvery grey bodies moving before I dove off the rocks, getting in the water first. While everyone in The Guard swam, only those of us pledging for the first time had anything to prove.

The inky-black water surrounding me hid silvery bodies darting around. They brushed against me, skin like neoprene, swimming in front, behind, churning the water to actually move me along. I stayed with them as long as I could, reluctant to give up my primo spot for something as ordinary as air. When I finally surfaced, a dolphin with skin brighter than the others stopped; raised her head and stared. It felt like she recognized me, but I knew I'd never seen her before.

I'd heard of her, of course. White dolphins played a large role in Pinhold mythology. Based on her size and age, she was the elusive albino born the month before me. I never believed she actually existed.

She dove back under the water and I followed without taking enough oxygen. Underwater, she nudged me forward, and as I picked up speed, she came alongside me. Her smooth movement created a slipstream, a pocket in the liquid that let me stay right against her. I focused on staying with her as we moved in front of the crowd and lost track of all the other dolphins, and people too.

Underwater, time passed differently. I didn't realize that I had forgotten to breathe until I landed next to the dolphin on some jagged rocks, gasping for air. I couldn't move my body, no matter what I tried.

A sharp fragment of rock dug into that soft indented space behind my ear. Blood—the dolphin's and mine— mixed in the water between us, and she looked wan, instead of pearly white. I got worried. She flopped her tail a few times, unable to get off of the rock. When I moaned in pain, she stopped doing that and looked right at me with one eye. I blinked for a second, breaking the stare when I felt her pulse. I knew it was there. It came through my skin and into my bones, right to the spot that hurt the worst. At once, the blood clotted and the pain stopped. But, I was still stranded too far away for anyone near the bonfire on the beach to see.

Then, Blake sprang from the ocean like a dolphin with wings, or at least that's what it looked like to me. I tried to smile, but my lips wouldn't move and since my eyes weren't all the way open, he set up for mouth-to-mouth. If the situation were reversed, I would have too.

Gently he began to push on my chest, counting to thirty. Like the dolphin's pulse, his touch went right through me. Once I could move again, I didn't want to. Blake went forward with his plan, adjusting my throat carefully before touching his mouth on mine. At that moment, my attraction shifted from neutral to positive.

A magnetic reversal had reset my internal compass on a molecular level and I needed to kiss him for my very existence to make sense. I felt his shock, and then his interest as he shifted gears from rescue to romance, kissing me back until we heard Mica's panicked yell and froze in place.

"Mica, stop, I'm fine. It's a scratch," I said, struggling to sit up on the rocks. I showed him the roughened skin on my shoulder that was nothing worse than a surfing thrash. Looking into his identical silver eyes, I clicked to convince him I wasn't the one who needed help.

The dolphin wriggled on the rocks next to me, chirping, clicking and whistling in a very stressed-sounding tone. The dolphins who answered her calls followed her out of the water and on to the beach. Everyone who had completed the swim, as well as those waiting on land for the party, worked furiously to get them off the black lava sand that tended to scratch skin.

Getting each dolphin back in the water meant lifting at least four hundred pounds of struggling muscle, turning them around and carrying them until the bay was deep enough for them to swim. It was noisy and terrifying, but the other dolphins were getting the help they needed, so I gave all of my attention to the one beside me.

"Guys, help me with her, please!" I said to Blake and Mica, putting my arms around her in order to prevent her from hurting herself more. Though her skin felt like the sturdy rubber of a wet suit, I saw from the scrapes already on her that it was as sensitive as mine.

"On three," Mica said. He and Blake had moved on either side of the dolphin and had wedged their arms underneath her body to protect her from the scraggy surface as we pushed her back into the sea.

We carried her until we were waist deep, releasing her as soon as it was possible. Then, we all collapsed in the water, reeling from the stress of so many dolphins beaching on the sand at once. She took a second to nuzzle us, showing gratitude. But we couldn't stay in the happy moment for long. We needed to help the other dolphins, whose clicks and whistles had gone from playful to stressed; the ones safe in the water, as well as those stuck on the sand.

Now that I was practically on top of her, I realized she was a rare albino dolphin, not just a light-skinned one. The albino swam away from the rocks, calling the other dolphins towards her and out to sea. The ones who could turn, did so and followed, leaving twenty or so gray animals struggling in the shallows. Moving as quickly as possible, I ignored my own pain and ran to the others with Blake and Mica. We worked with everyone on the beach to turn the rest of the dolphins and get them back in to the ocean; happy when they finally moved to a deeper, safer part of the sea.

Before swimming from sight, the albino turned, eyeing me just like Mica had done, as if to check that I was okay. Seemingly satisfied, she turned and went to the open ocean with her pod. I trudged onto the beach, elated that we had managed to save them all, but exhausted and confused too.

Moments later, surrounded by concerned partygoers, I sat on a bench and bit my lip to keep from crying. The scrape on my shoulder didn't hurt when it had happened, but it sure burned during a thorough cleaning with peroxide. Billy produced a first-aid kit and used the lights on the golfie to see the damage. When I could no longer hold back the tears, Celeste pushed her way in and applied the liquid bandage herself.

"Epic First Night, huh?" Mica joked, attempting to break the tension. He looked over at Billy for confirmation. I didn't noticed when I first saw Billy that day, but Blake and Mica had both grown taller than him since the last time Billy had been home.

"I'd say. You have mad dolphin calling skills, Cami," Billy said, giving me a gentle fist bump while Celeste continued to cover the scratches on my back.

"Well, yeah, as long as the dolphins—and Cami—are fine," said Blake, eyes flashing to mine in the firelight.

"Not totally fine," I said, flicking my red plastic cup to make the point.

"Boys, I think Cami needs another beer," Celeste interrupted, "and so do I." I giggled nervously. I wasn't much of a beer drinker, and neither were the boys. But it was a bit of a tradition on first night, and after everything that had happened with Blake, I needed the liquid courage.

Mica and Blake fell over each other moving towards the keg with Billy, while they talked about the crazy speed and size of the pod that had joined us for the swim. Celeste finished bandaging and went from serious caretaker to giggly fangirl. "That was amazing!" she squealed, right into my ear.

With her russet curls bouncing with excitement, it was hard to remember Celeste was a serious research scientist.

"You mean embarrassing," I said. "How am I ever going to make The Guard if some rocks and a foot of water almost made me drown?"

"Cami, that was hardly a drowning. What happened out there??"

"I'm not sure. As soon as I dove in, I got carried up in their wakes, or something that felt like it," I guessed, remembering the feeling of the albino dolphin moving me through the waves.

"You were in a slipstream?" Celeste asked, giddy with impressed surprise.

I smiled. "I think so, if that's what it's called when they carry you along."

"Wow, that's how moms carry their calves in the water before they can swim fast enough to keep up. I can't believe so many of them came—and then beached. And, then we got them all back in the water so fast! Why did you swim up on the rocks, anyway?" Celeste looked at me with concern.

I paused, furrowing my forehead, considering her question. "I guess I got turned in the wrong direction? I don't remember much, except that I didn't want to come up for air and leave the slip stream."

"Maybe you passed out under water?" she asked, looking concerned. "Either way, that albino saved you. Isn't that a sign of fortune, according to the Island legends?"

I nodded. Just spotting an albino was considered very good luck, but being rescued by one? I couldn't begin to imagine what the Elders would interpret that to mean. Many of the Elders worshipped the sea, instead of one of the more typical American religions. If they couldn't see it, they didn't believe it. My grandparents were the opposite. Everything was a sign, a feeling; open to interpretation based on many silent factors that only they understood.

"Definitely a good omen for a great summer," I said, feeling optimistic in spite of the pain.

"That made my summer and it's only solstice," Celeste said dreamily, sounding more like a little kid who'd spotted a unicorn than a research scientist.

"Seeing that dolphin? Don't you work with them, like all day and every day?" I asked.

"Yes, but that one's an anomaly. Some scientists can't handle them, because they mess up statistics, but I love the unusual ones. And that's the first albino I've ever seen. In case it's the last, I want to enjoy it. Have you ever seen her before?"

I shrugged, thinking back to my childhood. "When I was little, an albino used to come up to our docks with her pod. I don't know if it's the same one or not, but when we were six, they passed a law to prevent people from feeding the dolphins. They felt like we were being mean and they didn't understand, and they stopped coming."

"There was some concern they were forgetting how to hunt and, instead, learning to beg for food, which wasn't good for them," Celeste explained. "Let's chalk it up to a magical First Night that leads to a whole bunch of Surf Carnival wins. And that kiss with Blake," she said, switching gears, "was beyond amazing!"

"You saw that?" I said, cringing. "He was going to give me mouth-to-mouth, and I kissed him. I'm such an idiot." I pulled my knees up and covered my face in them to hide the blush on my skin.

"That may have been his, 'I'm Blake, I'm so responsible' plan. Or... what if the CPR thing was just an excuse?" Her eyes twinkled, but I felt confused.

"He would have done the same thing for anyone," I said, still blushing.

"You're kidding, right?" Celeste laughed, in the way older girls with boyfriends could—like they knew something we didn't. "Cami, haven't you noticed the way he stares at you?" she said, stroking my hair.

Well I did. A bit. Earlier that night, he surprised me when we were getting in the golf truck that brought us to First Night.

When I'd walked out from my door, Blake had whistled. He'd lived next door to me for years, and that was the first time I'd ever seen that kind of look on his face.

"Wow," he said with a wink of his turquoise eye. The other, his right one, was half that same startling blue and half grayish silver.

My twin brother Mica, who had followed me out the door, had laughed. He'd had to wait while I'd taken a ridiculous amount of time with my clothes and hair.

"That makes you one self-centered bastard," Mica said, punching Blake on the arm. They were friends. Best friends. And Mica was alluding to the fact we looked similar enough to Blake to pass for cousins when we wanted to fool the daily visitors who came to beach to surf.

Ours was a small island with a shallow gene pool. Endless summers gave everyone the same sun-kissed, tanned glow, even before you factored in the many sets of identical twins that comprised an unusually high portion of our population.

Blake was the poster child for life here on Pinhold. A blond, tan, sixteen-year-old swimming god featured in the ad campaign for this year's Surf Carnival. The competitive swimming and surfing event drew international pros from both sports to our tiny town.

Blake's twin, Kaleb, had left Pinhold when we were thirteen. He'd been my best friend, just as Blake was my twin brother Mica's.

Blake and Kaleb were mirror twins—identical polar opposites. Blake's right eye matched Kaleb's left, Kaleb's nose hooked the tiniest bit right, while Blake's had the same angle going the other way. They had corresponding crescent birthmarks in exactly the same place on their left and right knees.

Like all magnetic objects going in the same direction, they repelled each other. Blake dove head first into island life while Kaleb rejected almost everything. He hated how Blake and Mica got serious about joining The Guard, the island governing body. Part police force, part town council, part surf rescue club, The Guard ruled over Pinhold. They valued secrecy, and you were either in or out.

For years, I sided with Kaleb, dreaming of escape to faraway places with people who cared about other things besides swimming and surfing. But somewhere along the way, I began to enjoy life on the island. I still wanted to escape, but I'd gone and dragged myself into Surf Competitions, which made Kaleb feel as if I'd turned my back on him.

We'd all fought and Kaleb went in search of trouble bad enough to get him sent off for good. He snuck over to the tiny island to see Pinhold's secret symbol for himself. The ancient pin supposedly stood straight up on a tiny tip, balanced magnetically on a rock in the middle of our archipelago.

Kaleb had doubted its existence, and went to the little island to see it. He'd gotten kicked off of Pinhold for his trouble, and I'd joined Mica and Blake and the others in training to get in and serve The Guard someday. Tonight's ceremony was the official beginning of that possibility – the annual summer kick off called First Night.

Celeste's giggles brought me back to the present. "Billy said no one would ever mistake you for Mica again," she confided, and I shook my head. He might have been Blake's older brother but he often acted like mine.

"That's so embarrassing," I whispered, hiding my face in my hands. My face reddened because the older boy had called attention to the fact that, in spite of being different genders, Mica and I had passed for identical twins, what with his long surfer boy hair and my complete lack of girlish curves.

Still, tonight I'd worked hard on getting the right look. I'd skipped my basic racing tank and board shorts, pairing a white bikini and red tank with a denim skirt that looked a bit tight in the right way.

Even so, Blake hadn't exactly gone after me romantically. He attempted to rescue me--an important difference.

"I've got you," he'd said locking his arms around me, holding on just tightly enough to keep me safe. Being that close to him usually made me slightly nauseas, like nails on the chalkboard. He disrupted my equilibrium, and not in a good way.

"No," I blushed. "He didn't initiate it at all. He wouldn't. That's just not what we're like. There's zero attraction there," I explained, the words sounding false even to my own ears. "He's always with Mica...which makes him practically my brother...like our third twin. I doubt he even sees me as a girl. In any event, I'm not interested in someone my family decided I should be with before I was even a person. It's a trap. He's a trap. And someday I want to leave Pinhold, see a bit of the world."

"A six-foot-four, blond trap that frequently practices chivalry," she pointed out. "Sounds like a trap I would gladly fall in."

"You have Billy, and you're choosing to be here. As soon as I can, I'm going to leave." Celeste had gone to college, left her hometown to go study oceanography, which was her dream. On Pinhold, dreams didn't matter. Service did. Those of us lucky enough to descend from the ten founding families were stuck in a bit of a gilded cage. In exchange for at least one year of service on the island, we were gifted land to build a house and a portion of a living fund that could sustain us as we extended a year of service into a lifetime.

For people like Billy, with specific passions, college and even graduate school was encouraged and even paid for. But he was here now, doing his medical residency on the Pinhold and lining up to take over the medical center when the doctor who currently ran it retired.

Blake's future was as planned out as Billy's. He'd been groomed as Stoney's replacement since birth, and he'd embraced his future every day. He trained hard, never complained and seemed to take energy from Kaleb's utter disdain. Blake's genuine appreciation for island life had grown on me, to the point that I almost admired his ability to accept his future and his fate with joy.

Almost.

But I couldn't do the same for myself. My own family's expectations loomed larger than the ocean. They expected me to follow in my grandmother's footsteps and stay and take over training, grow into a leader.

They even wanted me to marry Blake. Legitimately. It was said as a joke, but like many ideas repeated over and over again for laughs, that one was serious. And it didn't matter that I'd never demonstrated any interest in him that way. They just didn't care. It was best for our families, and the island, and therefore it was best for me.

I loved my grandmother and felt nothing but respect for the way she'd lived her life. Her relationship with my grandfather was incredible and their love was inspiring. But just because she married her boy next door didn't mean I had to. Repeating her story was not my meant-to-be.

I resented that my opinions didn't matter, but I kept that spark of anger inside. I used it to fuel my workouts, to race swim faster, compete harder. I was earning a ticket out, and I promised myself that when the time came, I'd make all the important choices for myself.

Blake was their choice, not mine. Not before tonight. Which was why tonight's kiss had me so unraveled.

"Earth to Cami! Where'd you go?" Celeste asked, waving a hand in front of my eyes.

"Here," I said, swallowing my uncertainty behind a small smile.

"Wasn't that ceremony all about you joining The Guard?" she asked cautiously, looking over her shoulder to make sure no one heard her prying.

"Yes, well, year of mandatory service and all that. I've already gotten on Beach Patrol for the summer. Getting in The Guard would be the best place to spend the rest of the year."

Celeste nodded, looking at me like she had a million questions. That made two of us. Because so did I. I hadn't expected to feel so much for the evening, and the event. The connection to history and to the spiral of time surprised me. It affected me almost as much as calling the dolphins, and swimming with them to shore.

I felt pulled to them magnetically, connected by history and fate. I'd grown up with the myths, but they never resonated before tonight. Now, I understood that there was some sort of a connection. It was subconscious, innate, and undeniable, triggered by the events of the night.

"That was mostly dedicating myself to the ocean. And I'm comfortable with committing to that." And I was. All of us are born of the ocean, but some of us remember it more. I was one of those. That wouldn't change, no matter where I went. But there were lots of oceans, and I needed to explore more than just this one.

"So don't worry about committing to anything. Why can't you just enjoy this Cami? It's perfect here." She sighed and I heard the appreciation and the wonder in the sound. I got it. I knew Celeste came from a landlocked city somewhere down south. Billy often joked that she'd looked up where he came from before agreeing to their first date. But she was choosing to be here. I didn't have a choice.

I shrugged and bit my lip. "For me, it's a trap. And Blake is the bait."

"Oh please. Are you really going to let a bunch of old jokes keep you from something you want? How did you feel when you kissed him?"

"I...I..." I stopped, stuttering. I felt like I had with the dolphins.

"Like I was in the right place at the right time?" It wasn't a question. And I didn't know why I phrased it as one. I hated that insincere uncertain uptalking thing some girls did when they didn't want to own their feelings. I swallowed hard and tried again. "More... alive."

Celeste looked at me with one eyebrow raised. "Then grab onto that Cami, play with it, and see what happens. Giving up something that feels good just because other people want it for you is just as foolish as only doing what you're told. Just play."

My brain spun a bit, trying to make sense of her words. Her valid points released a pressure in my chest and I took a deep breath for the first time since coming out of the water. I had more questions, needed more advice. But there wasn't time.

"Shush," she whispered. And I heard the boys coming back. I wondered if my speech had convinced her because I hadn't convinced myself. About Blake or The Guard. The Guard I could still take or leave, but there was nothing neutral about how I felt when I looked at Blake.

I flirted, laughed, danced, and drank until the beer didn't taste terrible anymore. This was a night to forget about training and celebrate. I'd have the whole rest of the summer to make up for it. Even the Elders stayed and had a beer or two, but they'd left after a half hour or so.

Everyone left was closer to my age, and they were in no hurry to leave. Blown away by the evening's events, I needed to let the energy out too.

Since I'd never made it past a sip or two before, I'd been buzzed since the first cup of beer. After the second, I got dizzy, giggling and dancing around, passing out sticks and marshmallows. Blake watched me move around the circle. I saved him for last, because I felt embarrassed about what I'd done on the rocks, and I wasn't sure what to say to him. I handed him the last stick and nudged him over to the fire.

"Um, Cami, isn't this stick a bit short? Are you trying to set me on fire?" he asked, smiling and flashing dimples in the amber glow. My jaw dropped at his choice of words because they had a few very different meanings, given what just occurred.

I gave myself a mental whack in the head and though back to what Celeste had said. Blake was flirting with me, and I just stood there silently, frozen, and possibly drooling. I needed to get it together.

I smiled back, glad the night hid the blush on my cheeks from the thoughts he'd put into my head with just that one comment.

"Maaaybeeee," I said, drawing out the word because let's face it; I was so flustered I was lucky to come up with one. I took the stick back, pulled three marshmallows from the bag, and pushed them down one at a time.

I walked around to the other side of the bonfire, where only a couple of people sat. I reached my arm toward the flame, stumbling, and the marshmallows went directly into the fire, the flames way too close to my hand. Blake grabbed me immediately, and pulled me away, rescuing me again.

"Death wish tonight, Cami?" he asked, blowing out the charred treats. He ran his fingers over my arm to make sure it wasn't burned and I held my breath until he finished. My skin was just a little warm from the brush with fire, but it had gotten positively hot by the time his inspection was done. I pouted and licked my lips, looking longingly at the stick. "Fine," he said, rolling his eyes. "Let's go get another."

He turned back to the edge of the clearing. I recovered my beer and followed him to the tree line, still holding the short stick with the blackened marshmallows in my other hand. He'd pulled a thin sapling from a low hanging branch, and was stripping the leaves quickly, but not fast enough for me.

Too impatient to wait, I took a bite from what I had, pulling my lips away when they burned. To cool my mouth down, I sipped from the cup in my hand, and tried not to make a face at the comment. "Beer and burnt marshmallows? Two great things that aren't great together." He laughed, taking the cup from my hand.

"They are, actually," I said, licking a bit of sticky white stuff off the right side of my mouth. He watched me intently, his look even sweeter than the candy.

"Try it," I offered, stepping forward and putting the stick to his lips. He leaned in, closed his eyes, tilted his head, and touched his lips to the same exact place where mine had been.

I breathed in, smelling the smoke from the fire in between us and enjoying the moment. Until he squinted his eyes, pursed his mouth, shook his head, and totally broke my trance.

"Way too burnt," he said, scratching his tongue on his teeth to get rid of the taste. I loved the way he touched my face as I leaned toward him. His eyes changed again, as he stared right at me, running his fingers down my cheek, then my neck. His thumb passed over my collarbone, and then slowly, so slowly, he gripped my neck, right under my ear where I'd gotten hurt a few hours before. Drugged with anticipation, and buzzed, I felt no pain. I closed my eyes, aching with anticipation, hopeful he would kiss me again. Then, he stroked the skin behind my ear.

"Ouch," I protested, before I could stop myself.

Acting quickly, I leaned up and kissed him, distracting from the worry that had crossed his face. When our lips parted, he looked more shocked and concerned than turned on. Crisis averted, I sent a silent thank you to the Universe and hoped my cut would take care of itself.

two

"BUT, BUT, BUT that's impossible! I'll miss the Ocean Swim!" I counted to ten in my head and still couldn't contain the small sob that erupted.

"You're lucky you're not out the whole summer, Cami Coane," Doc said, using my full name in that annoying way grownups did. He was none too gentle putting the last stitch in my head. It hurt more than getting the stupid cut.

I tried to stay quiet through the stitches. My mom was in the room, freaking out enough without me showing her I was in pain.

"Or worse! God, Cami, anything could have happened! Maybe you're not ready for the Surf Carnival this year," Mom said. I worked hard not to roll my eyes at her. She was the only person on Pinhold who seemed to hate to swim.

"Mom, I told you, it didn't even hurt when it happened. It's a tiny cut. Billy checked me out and made sure I was okay." I looked at Doc. "Isn't he here? He'll tell you. I was fine. With everything else going on, it was really no big deal."

"Yes, I heard you called the dolphins. I also heard that a bunch of them beached themselves," said Doc.

My mom's eyes widened. We hadn't talked about last night. She'd come in my room to check on me in the morning, found blood on my pillow, and dragged me to see Doc.

"Cami, tiny cuts don't require stitches. And, any head injury is serious. Especially at a party, where there's usually a very specific and not so smart reason things don't hurt when they happen," Doc said in that authoritative voice I'd heard my entire life. I clamped my eyes down tight in an effort to quell the eye roll that was desperate to escape. I couldn't do that to Doc, who was at least as instrumental as my parents in engineering my existence.

"I wasn't drinking when it happened—really! It was during the swim. I was on the rocks with the dolphin, and I didn't even realize anything had happened," I insisted.

"All the same, if you swim or get your hair wet this week, these stitches will dissolve too soon," Doc said. "And I'll have to shave your head to put in the other kind."

"No showers?" This time, I did actually squeal. My crazy mess of amber waves required constant conditioning to keep knot-free. In a week, I'd be halfway to dreadlocks!

"Shower cap. Dry shampoo," said a welcomed voice by the door. "Hi, Cami, Lydia, Doc."

"Billy," my mom said, smiling. "Is this what they teach in medical school these days?"

"No, ma'am. I did a practicum in the ER. Saw a lot of injuries like…" he trailed off, caught, tangling us both in the net.

"Exactly!" said my mom, shooting an angry glare my way. "I wish someone would have explained that to my daughter at the party. If Thomas were here, instead of on some rickety research boat in the middle of the Pacific, this would have been handled properly last night."

Thoughts of my father had her flipping from fussing to fretting. It amazed me she and my dad had ever come together. He was an avid swimmer and waterman - not competitively anymore, but he still worked in The Guard when he wasn't teaching archaeology at a college on the mainland. I cursed the research trip he was on now. I knew this particular opportunity was the reward for ten years of research and grant proposals, but it sucked to have him gone.

"I was there, ma'am. Checked her over and cleaned her up myself," Billy said. "She acted fine and her head wasn't bleeding at the time."

My mom paused; trust in Billy competing with the anxiety she'd had our whole lives. All mothers worried, but mine would bind us up in bubble wrap if it were possible. Every tiny scratch required a visit to the doctor; colds meant full check-ups, and anything more serious than that included blood tests. She had a soft spot for Billy, like all the grownups on the Island, because he'd acted like a surrogate big brother to us all.

He taught us to surf and swim, ride and run. For ten years, we were only allowed out of the house if Billy came too. Luckily, he patiently led us around until college took him off-Island. It took Mom months to let us go anywhere after that.

"Isn't there a protocol with The Guard for head injuries? Why wasn't it followed?" she asked.

"It was, ma'am. Cami got up, walked, and talked right away. We checked her vitals for signs of concussion and none were there. The only visible injuries were scrapes on her shoulders, which she could have gotten with any big wave crashing her onto shore. I understand the cut must have been deep, but there was no indication of the injury at the time. I wrote up a report of the incident," Billy said, offering it to her.

Mom grabbed the folder from his hand and opened it with a huff.

"I know it's scary, Lydia, but if Billy says she was okay, she was. Member of The Guard or not, you would have never hired him to work at the hospital if he wasn't a fantastic doctor," Doc spoke again; reminding us he was in the room. "But no swimming for you for at least a week," he said sternly, pointing a finger at me.

I worked hard to keep from crying because, swimming was as important as breathing to me. Even more importantly, the first Surf Carnival event was tomorrow, and I wasn't going to get to participate. "So, no Ocean Swim," I said. "Ca-can I at least stay on Beach Patrol?"

Doc and my mother exchanged a look. Since she'd gone from his most obsessive patient to his hospital manager, they'd developed a good working relationship and a shorthand. She'd taken over Island General when it got too big. She would go by whatever he said, but he would get her approval first.

She gave an almost imperceptible nod and Doc nodded. "You can stay on Beach Patrol. I'll call Stoney."

I sighed, relaxing for the first time since arriving at Doc's office. Whatever they wanted me to do, I would do it—as long as I didn't have to give up actually getting paid to sit on the beach and watch the water with my friends. I'd waited for this job for sixteen years, and I wasn't giving up the red bikini, the whistle, or that tall white beach chair.

All the citizens on Pinhold had to dedicate a minimum of year of service to the island, and most dedicated their whole lives. Getting into The Guard was the ultimate assignment, the pinnacle of Pinhold society. We'd been born and bred for this, but we weren't all expected to make it in. I had to make sure that I was one who did. Because then, whatever else happened, I would always know it had been my choice. And I needed it to be.

"Work. Home. No two-way communication devices; until the Ocean Swim," my Mom said, as she brought down the gauntlet at home, later. "The only reason you're not grounded longer is because Doc and Billy came to your defense."

The twitching muscle above his right eye indicated to anyone that Mica was annoyed. But, because of our twin link, I felt and heard and saw so much more—even though he didn't say a word. It had always been this way between us. My very first memories were images seen through his eyes. This was true for all the sets of twins our age. We didn't link outside of our own sibling, but we'd learned early on that each pair could communicate that way. And we'd managed to keep that fact between the eight of us for years.

Our parents had known about it when we were small, but testing had been inconclusive and no different than twins elsewhere in the world. Now that we were older, we all knew it wasn't normal for everyone, but it was normal for us. So, in an unspoken pact, we never talked of it, not even amongst ourselves.

The emotion behind the images was impossible to disguise. Over the years—especially lately—we'd learned to control what we shared a bit better. When calm, we could limit it to words; silent telepathic text messages that conveyed just the right amount of information. The unfiltered images transmitted every layer of joy, pain and confusion were too raw. They shared too much information, had too much ability to influence, like on First Night. We'd even learned, just recently, to keep certain thoughts to ourselves.

Mica's anger in the moment meant he wasn't filtering, and I felt his thoughts as clearly as my own.

First, he considered asking why he was grounded too, since he didn't technically do anything. Then, he decided to accept the sentence, because he felt guilty about not realizing how hurt I'd actually been. I silently thanked him for not fighting Mom.

No two-way communication devices, I said. Too bad she can't take away our brains.

Mica laughed out loud.

"Mica, your sister almost DROWNED. This is no laughing matter. You didn't take her to the hospital or even wake me up when you got home!"

Poor Mom didn't have any idea why we were really laughing. She'd never caught on to our special communication skills, and we never felt the need to tell her about them. For a short while, when we were very young, she'd suspected and there had been tests. We'd intentionally wrecked the results and she had never questioned it.

"Mom, he wanted to call an ambulance," I said, rising to my brother's defense. "I'm the one who said no. Go ahead and ground me for having an ACCIDENT. But don't punish Mica, too!"

Thank you, but no, Mica said silently. To our Mom he just nodded, accepting the punishment.

Though the sentence had been handed down, the lecture wasn't over.

"Be safe. Don't do anything stupid. Take care of each other. House rules. Sound familiar?" Mom glared at us. Her anger always came out in this shaky, teary tone that typically transformed my annoyance to shame. "Can you honestly tell me that what happened last night didn't involve you each breaking at least one of them?"

Was that a rhetorical question or one that required an answer? I chose silence, considering it was my last statement that had started her shrieking. Mica chose silence, too, but then he was her favorite for a reason. He knew instinctively when to push and when to back down, whereas I could never get that right at all.

"I've been to those parties; I know what goes on. If your cut barely hurt, then I'm going to guess alcohol had everything to do with your mutually-impaired judgment."

With that, she held her hand out for our iPhones and stormed from the room.

I sat on the dock with my father's fishing rod, wishing he were here to help me catch dinner like he usually would on a summer night. I didn't have the patience to sit still for this alone, but I liked the time he and I had spent waiting on fish together. So far, I'd pulled two salmon; nothing to sneeze at, but not enough for a family meal. I hoped a fresh-caught dinner might score some points with my mom, but on my own I never had as much luck as I did with Dad.

My father always put my mother's histrionics in perspective, trusting me at a very young age with information about what they had gone through before Mica and I came to be. The Island had been broke; most people my parents' age were moving away and everyone who stayed had similar issues getting, and staying, pregnant. So The Guard decided to sell offshore drilling rights in the Back Bay, and, as they'd hoped, Pinhold experienced a bit of a boom. Suddenly, there were tourists and jobs, and things began to look up again. Then, one of the platforms exploded, causing the black oil to flood the bay, and we spent the next twenty years trying to undo the environmental and legislative damage.

That's how the Surf Carnival came to be. It was an ancient ritual practiced as kind of a coming-of-age on Pinhold. While the oil rig was up, some of the Mainer workers began to participate, and interest grew as more people became aware of the challenging swimming and surfing opportunities the contest offered.

"Top five," Mica said out loud.

He'd snuck up behind me on the deck, and sat next to me. He'd clearly been blocking his thoughts since I hadn't sensed him at all. It was almost time for the sun to set—a special time of day for everyone on Pinhold; Mica especially. Our dock was one of the best places to watch a sunset on the Island. The glow here lasted for a full two hours in the summer while light sank slowly over to the other side of the world.

Mica grabbed Dad's rod and handed me the lure to thread a worm. Though he was inching past six-feet, he always had me thread his worms when no one else was around. I hung one over his head, hoping he would scream.

"For the hundredth time, I am not afraid. I just don't want to kill them for no reason," he argued, using the same words every time the topic came up.

"It's Darwinian—survival of the fittest," I argued.

"I don't need the fatal services of a lower life form to secure food," he insisted. "But I can't use nets this close to shore when the tide is low, and I don't want Mom to find me out too far in the water. She might consider it a jail break."

I'm sorry, I said silently, counting on the telepathic communication to convey my regrets more sincerely than spoken words.

"You're the only one I'm not mad at," he said. Images of Mom, Blake, and himself flickered from his brain to mine.

Oh no—Blake. I'd been deliberately trying not to think about the kiss around Mica, not knowing how to explain it. Blake was his best friend. It was possible that by kissing him, I'd stepped in someplace I didn't quite belong.

"I'm mad at myself. I can't believe Blake got to you first. I was too focused on my swim when I should have been more aware of you. I deserve to be grounded just for that." He turned to me, genuinely upset. "I'm sorry."

"Mica, just because we shared a womb, doesn't mean we have to share every single experience, all the time," I said, relieved that so far, the kiss had escaped mention.

"But you got hurt. I've been thinking about it all day and I can't figure it out. For the first time ever, I didn't feel your pain. Remember when I broke my arm?"

I nodded, picturing little Mica on a huge surfboard. He'd wiped out in our first competition as Nippers, the kiddie competition in the Surf Carnival. His very first wave had kicked him off the board, headfirst into the shallow break. I'd been on a walk with my Dad a half-mile down the beach when I forced him to turn around to get Mica. Of course, our thoughts were linked but the pain came through differently.

"I really didn't know my head was that bad? I barely felt it. The scrapes on my arms hurt more," I said, which wasn't true, exactly. The pain had been intense until the dolphin had…zapped me. Or something that felt that way. I surely couldn't explain when I didn't understand it myself.

"Maybe it was all the extra endorphins from the swim? I stayed underwater longer than I ever have before, so maybe that, too?"

"Yeah, you beat the pants off me. I tried to keep up with the dolphins, but they were chasing you."

Dolphins, because of their playfulness and intelligence, were the symbol for our island. According to Island lore, they were our other halves, guarding the water as we did the land. Their health was a sign we were doing our job. Whenever they had issues, trouble came our way too. In many old stories, breachings occurred before the pin began to tilt. Dolphins were a sentinel species. What happened to them will happen to us, and what happened to us will happen to the rest of the world.

"It's just a myth. Dolphins come on the beach to chase food all the time. Did you see how many came to First Night? It's gonna be a good season."

I nodded, appreciating his optimism. "Except for me. I'm missing the Ocean Swim," I grumbled. "I'll have to place in every other event to get invited to join The Guard."

Mica snorted.

"Really? Cami, there's been someone in The Guard in our family the past twenty generations; they've been waiting on us for sixteen years. You'd have to pull a Kaleb and set fire to the lighthouse or something."

"Ha, ha," I said, cringing when Kaleb's name came up.

Before Kaleb started getting in trouble, he and I had been best friends, just like Mica and Blake. Kaleb had been my fellow explorer and observer, while our brothers pursued all the sea sports Pinhold offered. He had Blake to take on the role of family athlete, Pinhold leader. But that didn't work for me.

While my grandparents were proud of Mica, and expected him to do well and get in The Guard, I was the girl, and therefore responsible for my grandmother's legacy. So, I began to train, too. Kaleb supported me, at first. His sarcasm helped me swallow down the bitter pill of expectation, helped smooth my acceptance of a responsibility I hadn't wanted. But, the ocean and the exercise quickly won me over. I fell in love with riding waves and moving through water like I was born to.

And Kaleb had never forgiven me.

We'd been growing apart even before he'd left, but I never understood what made him so angry that made him target the lighthouse.

"Can we not?" I asked Mica, shaking the thoughts from my head. We had an unspoken agreement to not talk about Kaleb because the conversations never ended well. I got upset; Mica got mad. Blake couldn't deal at all.

"Get over it already," he joked, knowing immediately the intended humor did not at all hit home. Instead of filling with laughter, my eyes welled up with tears.

"How would you feel if Blake just moved off-Island and didn't come back?"

"You can't compare them, but it's been forever, Cami; and Blake is never leaving."

At least we could agree on that. Blake's commitment to following in Stoney's footsteps was something we often talked about. Blake couldn't wait to take on more responsibility here.

"Fine. Forget about me; have you noticed how just uttering Kaleb's name makes the vein above Blake's right eyebrow visibly pulse?" I asked. It was amazing how the same letters rearranged in a different way brought such a dramatic reaction. Blake and Kaleb's names were anagrams, just like Mica's and mine.

"Satan's in the spelling. Otherwise he's just Santa," Mica joked. A sudden tug on his line shifted his focus back to the water. "Caught something," he said, dropping the subject when his line gave a big tug.

I went right back on the dock after dinner, happy to enjoy the dark sky and the lapping waves without a fishing rod in hand. Mica was in the house, and I was blocking him, grateful for some alone time with the water I loved. Being by it was second best to swimming, but it was better than nothing. Even though I often found Pinhold to be too small, I loved living surrounded by the ocean and the bay. And it paid to have the same friends since the womb.

Alysha and Shayla knew exactly what time Mom would go back to work after dinner. Less than fifteen minutes after she left, they pulled their canoe up to our dock. Alysha jumped up, squealing and flapping so much that she missed the weathered wooden boards completely and landed in the water with a huge splash.

When she surfaced with pollywogs covering her usually perfect blond hair, Shayla and I laughed so hard we shook every boat on the dock. Alysha yanked her sister into the water, too. Luckily, there were plenty of extra towels and shorts and tees in the boathouse, and they were able to dry off and change.

With snacks at hand, Alysha jumped in with the questions. I was impressed she even lasted that long.

"It's was so romantic, Cami. He kissed you and woke you up; like Snow White. Or Sleeping Beauty," Alysha sighed.

She and Shayla were identical twins with completely different interests, but they managed to be friends, unlike Blake and Kaleb. Alysha chased glitter and drama, while Shayla had no time for anything that didn't make her stronger or smarter. The Princess and The Warrior. When they were together, Shayla indulged the whimsy and Alysha tamped down the bubbles. That's when I loved them best of all.

"I was awake," I protested. "Where were you guys, anyway?"

"We were turning the dolphins back into the water after you called them onto the beach," Alysha said, raising her eyebrows.

"She didn't call them onto the beach. She called them to the bay. She led them onto the beach," said Shayla. She was a stickler for facts and details, while her twin had a much more fluid relationship with truth.

"I didn't lead them anywhere," I objected. "One minute I was swimming with that white dolphin in front of the pod, and the next I opened my eyes and was stuck on the rocks.

"Cami, did you pass out?" Shayla asked, shocked. "Because an ambulance should have been called if you did. You know, because of Protocol." Shayla sounded almost angry.

"Did you talk to my mom? The same exact words came out of her mouth," I said. I knew Shayla wasn't mad, just passionate about the rules, but Alysha stepped in anyway.

"Probably in the same annoying tone. Who made you judge and jury?" Alysha asked her sister, her voice rising defensively. "Billy checked her out, and plenty of others gave second."

I shot Alysha a look of gratitude. But, my thanks were sent too early. She didn't care about helping as much as she wanted to get a different conversational hook on the line. "Besides, who cares about stupid Protocol," she said. That came as no surprise; she'd thrown down the gauntlet with The Elders and had steadfastly refused to take The Pledge to try to join The Guard.

While she could swim as well as the rest of us, she didn't want to, choosing instead to spend time on what she called 'artistic pursuits,' which usually meant hair and nails. She'd also made some jewelry to sell at the Surf Carnival to raise money for the Island Conservation fund, which was her way of protecting Pinhold without having to train on the beach all day. The Guard was letting it go this summer, because they didn't want any negativity bringing the rest of us down.

I admired her for standing her ground. Her fluffy hair and perfect smile disguised a will and soul as strong as steel.

Alysha started dancing around with her towel, humming some sort of waltz that sounded vaguely familiar. I raised an eyebrow towards Shayla when I couldn't place the tune.

"Sleeping Beauty," she said, rolling her eyes.

"How do you even remember that?" I asked.

"Believe it or not, it's the song for her alarm," Shayla said dryly. Alysha looked angry at this reveal, for all of ten seconds, before giggles took over.

"Speaking of clocks, it's curfew time," said Shayla, ever mindful of the rules. Alysha nodded and they gathered their things and hopped back into their canoe. As I disconnected their line from the dock, Alysha asked one more time about Blake.

I stalled and considered what to tell her.

Alysha was a great friend and could definitely be trusted. But, she had this ridiculous theory that if you told a secret to more than one person at the same time, it wasn't a secret anymore. Therefore, the receiver of information could spread the news without breaching trust.

I'd been caught in this logic trap of hers many times over the years and had stopped getting mad at her about it. But, I knew enough to be careful. And today, I was going to make this personality quirk of hers work for me.

"He didn't 'wake me up' at all. I kissed him," I said, whispering to add drama even though we were alone on the dock.

"What? You kissed Blake?" Alysha shrieked at the top of her lungs.

I half expected him to show up, she'd yelled his name so loud. Instead, a flock of sandpipers flew by, buzzing way too close to our heads. While Alysha and I ducked, Shayla stood her ground. She always was the bravest of the three of us, in action and conversation. So she went right back to it when we'd settled down.

"I'm impressed," said Shayla. "And surprised."

"Why Shay-Shay? It's like a movie. He rescues her, she kisses him to say thank you," Alysha sighed. "Like rewarding Prince Charming, or something."

"He didn't rescue her. She said she was awake, remember?" Shayla raised one eyebrow as if daring me to contradict her. When I didn't, Shayla nodded, and I knew the question would be dropped forever. "I didn't know you liked him like that," she said, making an odd face at me.

"Why on earth would she not like him?" Alysha said, totally unfazed. "He's hot, sweet, fast, hot, strong, smart. Did I mention hot?"

Alysha kept talking until Shay's fingers came into contact with her mouth, stopping the flow of adjectives.

"Yeah, you did, a couple times," said Shay.

"And, they're promised. So, it was only a matter of time."

Shayla looked at me, concern in her eyes. She wanted nothing more than to stay on-Island and join The Guard. But, we'd talked often enough of my interest in going off to see the world, and how getting involved with a Pinhold guy was something I wanted to avoid.

"You always said your grandparent's promises meant nothing," Shay said, in a clipped voice.

"Everything!" Alysha said, "He rescued her. That means it was true love's first kiss!" She sighed and swayed with the romanticism of it.

"Except since when is Blake your true love?" asked Shay.

And that's where she had me. She and I had plenty of debates about him because, she felt like he was the most perfect sample of human on this planet or any other. While she insisted her opinion was all about empirical evidence and not actually feelings, I often wondered. Did she like him? Would she hate me if I did, too?

I couldn't deal with any of this at the moment, so I pushed the question off. "He's not," I said, rolling my eyes. "It was just a tension breaker. Didn't mean anything," I said, getting away with protesting too much only because at that moment I waved them on their way. Out in the bay, the dolphins' joyful noises poked fun at my silent denial. My interest in Blake had done a one-eighty flip since First Night. I didn't know why, but denying it was becoming harder. With each moment that passed, the significance increased for me.

I just had no idea what was going on with him.

three

THE NEXT MORNING brought perfect weather for the opening of the Surf Carnival. I marched with a banner in the parade, but turned down the chance to be on the beach with the athletes. Alysha met me in the Pavilion, an empty open air building where contestants gathered before each event. She dragged me out the door and away from the sympathetic stares from my friends and family.

"No one would know if I just jumped in and swam," I grumbled. "I wouldn't need to win, I could stay on the down low."

"Like you would ever throw a race," Alysha said, rolling her eyes. "Why don't you put a black garbage bag over your head? You could stay anonymous and keep your boo-boo dry all at the same time!"

"Do you think that would actually work?" I wondered.

"Yes, if you wanted to drown!" She looked at me in dismay. "It's one race, Cami! You have three more competitions this summer and I know you will kick ass in all of them. Oh look, I see something that will make you feel better. Oh my god! Have you ever seen so many hotties all in one place?" Alysha squealed.

"Yup. Every year for the Ocean Swim," I said dryly. Just last week she and I made a wish list of which of the lifeguards from competing towns we hoped to see this year. Right in front of us was Ian Sentay, top surfer and beachwear model who reported on camera for some part of the ESPN family, at least according to the letters decorating the camera.

"Hello, ladies," he said, in a lazy Hawaiian lilt just made for surf reports. His family had been in surfing competitively even longer than mine.

"Sorry that you can't swim today, Cami. I was looking forward to reporting your win," he said, flashing his dimples and bright green eyes at me. His stare was so intense I felt a blush come to my face. I had no idea he'd even known my name. I felt Alysha pinching the skin on my lower back to try and get me to talk; when I didn't, she spoke up for me.

"Cami would say thank you, but her brain thinks she's swimming," Alysha said with her best smile.

"Alysha, right? Or Shayla?" Ian said. "Hey, can I interview you guys on camera?"

"Can I tell everyone about my jewelry fundraiser?" Alysha asked. Ian nodded and they got us set up. I guess if I couldn't swim, this was one way to remind everyone I was still in competition for the rest of the summer.

"We're here on Pinhold Island for the first event of the annual Surf Carnival, which goes on all summer. This is the annual Ocean Swim, which began as a traditional rite of passage for people who grew up on the Island. We're here with Cami Coane, who won the Junior Division of the Ocean Swim the past two years, but won't be swimming due to an injury. What makes the Ocean Swim such a challenging event here on Pinhold?" he asked, shoving the microphone in my face.

"The swimmers need to jump in from a fifteen foot drop, and swim against a very rough current," I explained.

Ian nodded to me and turned to the camera. "At least fifty percent of those in the water won't make it. And the people who grew up here have a decided advantage. How old were you when you first completed the course that our competitors will take today?"

"Eleven," I said, proud and embarrassed at the same time.

"Cami was the youngest girl in history," Alysha said proudly, making me smile. "I was fourteen. Which was considered late in my family," she joked, giving the camera a big grin. Go figure. She loved this. I just wanted it to be over.

"That's right. This is Alysha Anderson, whose identical twin, Shayla, is now expected to win the women's division. How do you feel about that, Cami?" he asked.

"I want Shay to win. We train together. We haven't had a hometown winner in seven years," I said.

"And who's swimming from your family?"

"My twin, Mica, and my grandmother," I said, smiling.

"For anyone who knows Surf Carnival history, or swimming history at all, Cami's talking about Ronnie Strick, the two time Olympic women's swimming champ who was born here on Pinhold. Good luck to your families," Ian said, thanking me, and making a 'cut' sign to the cameraman.

"Your grandmother is fierce. I'm a big fan," he said.

"Hey! What about the jewelry?" Alysha said, interrupting my train of thought. She held out her arm with the merchandise for sale. "They're to raise money for the Pinhold Conservation fund!"

"I'm sorry, Love," Ian, said, looking appropriately and adorably sad. "I'll tell you what? I'll buy a few and mention it as soon as I have a chance. Can they tweet you to buy?"

Alysha nodded and made the exchange, while I bounced up on my toes to see where everyone was. Once finished, she moved into typical Alysha bossiness. "Let's move. Hurry up! Five hundred swimmers are about to trample us running down these steps."

Conversation became impossible as the swimmers descended in the traditional Surf Carnival formation. Strict lines and paced marching seemed at odds with the event, but this tradition had stood a long time. Mica, Blake, and Shayla led three orderly lines down the middle of the steps, behind a small band of drummers and water pipe players that would hopefully call the dolphins to join the swim. That always made the crowd really excited, and we saw it as good luck.

The men's heat was first. Peering through the crowd, I looked for Blake and found him standing with Mica in the front row. That put them at the front edge of the cliff when it was time to jump in. But, the competition didn't start until everyone was actually in the water. I rubbed at the crescent of stitches behind my ear, frustrated to be watching from the sidelines. Just as the Master of Ceremonies blew the whistle, a pod of dolphins came charging towards the beach, which made it all that much harder to bear. As the cliff diving began, the pod kept a bit off the shore, steering clear of people. But then, as everyone tumbled into the start place, they jumped and played, showing off to the roaring crowd and getting everyone really hyped up for the race.

One of the many challenges in this race was starting from a still position—the dives didn't count, and the swimmers had to tread water before the kickoff.

The start whistle blew. Mica and Blake immediately burst from the water into competitive butterfly strokes. In asynchronous motion, one above the water while one was below; they flew ahead of the pack.

The ocean turned into a swirl of bodies and froth fighting to swim through the waves that, while smaller on this side of the Island, were at least six-foot swells. While the crowd cheered and jumped, I tuned them out like I would have if I were swimming. I still couldn't believe I wasn't swimming. My grandparents were disappointed; especially Gram who'd spent so many hours training me. But, unlike my mother, they knew I hadn't been doing anything irresponsible to get my injury. I watched the race through Mica's eyes, wishing I were in the water, too.

In my head, I heard his calculations; decisions about which bodies he needed to pass, when to reserve his breath, when to pop out for maximum speed. Usually, I was too focused on my own race to really pay attention to his. So I tried to look at that as some sort of silver lining. He and Blake were in the lead, neck and neck, popping out of the water like the dolphins swimming offshore. I usually avoided watching Blake swim, but my eyes were drawn to him. I hadn't seen him since First Night, except for the two seconds when they were getting in line for today. We'd smiled shyly at each other, which seemed strange.

Watching Blake swim was a definite wet dream. He was gorgeous everywhere, but especially swimming. In his element, he moved so smoothly through the surface that water slicked off his skin. His determination to win was visible every time he broke the surface; today I thought that was sexy as hell. The swim cap that covered his hair only served to draw attention to the planes of his face, stilled in serene concentration that belied the competitive nature inside.

He was an aw-shucks easy-going kind of guy, except when it came to swimming. There, he was fiercely determined to win. At eighteen, he was one of the best in the state and a likely contender for the Summer Olympics in 2016. While that may have seemed far away and quite remote, Olympic athletes were quite common on our tiny Island, especially considering the size. We were born to swim; it was in our blood.

Today, I couldn't pull my eyes away, even when the guy who had won the last two years got in front of Mica. I watched each of Blake's motions with a new reverence: up and over, one arm at a time, three strokes on each side. He was hypnotic. Each rise of his chest showed off a million cut muscles working in tandem to propel him forward faster than most people in the world would ever swim no matter how hard they worked.

His long limbs and height and genetic predisposition to athletics made it a little easier for him. But his stamina and focus came from his own heart and hard work and I'd always admired him for that. Even now, as others struggled not to lose ground where the ocean pushed against him at every stroke, he managed to speed through.

"Earth to Cami. Cami . . . Cami!" Alysha yelled, smacking my head and disturbing my perfect view. I blinked for the first time in at least five minutes. I needed to get Blake off of my brain and focus on Shay.

"Drool much?" she asked, passing over the cucumber water she made for herself every day. I was busted. I blushed bright red and gulped down some of the drink.

"You and every other woman around here. Some of the men too, I think. He's like art in the water, isn't he?" She giggled, looking around. "But the girls' heat is starting. Look!"

I watched as Shay, my Gram, and a few hundred other women made their way from the cliffs into the water. All things being equal, they were expected to hit the shore five to ten minutes after the men. And, of course, that was just the winners. There would still be plenty of stragglers, and some who would need to be fished out of the race completely. I knew it was intimidating to race alongside my Gram. For most women who competed in the Surf Carnival, she was a personal hero.

In addition to winning almost all the swim contests around the world in her day, she had been one of the people who founded the Surf Carnival, at least the modern incarnation. She and Blake's grandfather had participated in one in Australia and realized the event would bring people and excitement to the Island all summer. That was a time when visitors were few and Islanders were leaving in droves because of the lack of jobs and opportunity. They'd brought the Surf Carnival here, arguing that we put on all the events during a summer, anyway, because they were identical to the tests for The Guard.

Years later we had summers full of events that drew the best competitors in ocean sports to Pinhold. Daily visitors came on the ferry and paid a great deal of money spend time on our beaches, and we had a thriving little Island economy. And it all came out of people finding out about us from the Surf Carnival.

Even now, Gram was a celebrity on the circuit. Her presence in the event today was a big deal and not just for me. That was why she was staying in the race, even when I couldn't swim. It added an extra bittersweet element, but I contained my disappointment out of respect for her.

We watched the women dive in and then as soon as the swimmers were out of our range of vision, Alysha and I ran to the other side of the Pavilion, taking the hidden trail in the brush instead of the beach steps crawling with Mainers. Beating the crowd, we stood on the jetty and waited for them to appear at the finish line.

Ten minutes later, and still in sync, Mica and Blake came to the end of the race within seconds of one another. But, this race was not finished in the water; they had to get onto the shore and get through the finish ribbon first. Rising out of the water, muscles bunched like Poseidon, Blake made it on the rocks first. But Mica ran faster, getting up the cliff and through the finish line first. The crowd cheered for them both, and they played to it before coming over together to find us.

Blake caught my hand and pulled me against him for a very wet, spinning hug. Feeling spontaneous and celebratory, cheered on by the cackles of the dolphins, who had joined in about thirty yards from shore, it seemed so natural to lean in and peck him on the lips. I didn't want to make a practice of it, but being on the sidelines for a race was fun for a change.

Alysha's happy cheer broke in, eventually, busting through the buzz linking my head, heart and lips. "Shay Shay! Shay Shay! Shay Shay!" Alysha screamed. "You're so close!" She was about to be the first girl to finish, on track to beat my time from last year. I caught the down stroke of her fully awesome butterfly, only fifty yards from the finish line, tracking her in the water while I passed a brief glance over all the swimmers to spot Gram. She was swimming at a nice clip, towards the back of the crowd. I watched her, impressed as always with her strength in the water.

Then I lost sight of Shay. She had gone underwater and I kept my eyes on the finish line expecting her to come across at any minute, but that didn't happen. We waited, impatiently, unhappy when the girl who had been closest behind her came in. Then I heard them: panicked dolphin sounds. Mica's brain broke into mine with an image of me lying on the rocks and an image of Shay in the race. In a flash, we both flew off the small outcrop of rocks where we'd been standing on the beach and we were both in the water, swimming against the tide of bodies fighting to move to our shore.

It took an extra minute for my eyes to adjust in the water, but Mica was right on it, zipping down thirty-feet to check something close to the bottom of the sea. I swam far enough from Mica to give us both a different point of view. On the outskirts of the race, I spotted an unusually shaped bump resting on the ocean floor. I sent the image to Mica's brain, and he swam directly to the correct location. By the time I joined him, he held a limp Shayla in his arms.

Together, Mica and I dragged her to the surface and onto the sand. Alysha reached us in seconds, even before The Guard members that had scrambled to search for her as well. She hugged her sister's body while Blake tried for the second time in a week to give CPR. Shayla's responsive breathing brought a short moment of relief, until we learned she was otherwise unresponsive. Wrapped in a towel and answering questions from The Guard, I couldn't remember exactly what happened. Just like when I went under for first night, my memory was blank. I didn't remember anything after getting into the water.

The beach quickly went crazy with lifeguards from all over, going back into the ocean. Shayla wasn't the only one who went down. They were searching the water for two boys from other towns on the coast who hadn't come up when expected. I blocked out everything except for Alysha, who understandably became more and more hysterical as it became obvious Shayla was not okay. Though I was dripping from head to toe, I hugged Alysha anyway. I tried to tell her things would all work out, but my words of comfort sounded as fake as they felt.

The dolphins keened way out in the ocean, their sound reverberating loudly on the beach, which was almost silent despite the hundreds of people milling around. I shut up, letting their poignant cries speak for me.

four

"I DIDN'T DO anything wrong!" I said to Billy. I knew I was whining. But I couldn't help it as he held the buzzers to my head. Because I had gone in the water for Shay, my stitches were compromised. They had to shave part of my head in order to put in the more permanent ones.

"It's not a punishment, Cami. You know I wouldn't do this if it wasn't absolutely necessary," he said. "Now, hold still."

I sat like a statue, holding my breath to trap the tears threatening to spill. Billy was making good on Doc's promise to shave my head if the stitches dissolved too soon.

I wished Alysha could be here. She would know exactly what to do to expose the cut and also leave me with some sort of style. But, she couldn't, because she was in the ICU on the other side of the hospital with her sister.

The doctors were trying to figure out why Shayla was breathing on her own, showed no other signs of injury, but was completely unresponsive. We'd all stood around in the waiting room for a few hours, until Doc had insisted that my cut had to be dealt with before infection had time to settle in. Mica came with me. They wanted to draw blood from both of us to rule out chemicals in the water that could have caused Shayla to go down. Like a caged bear,

Mica paced around the room, huffing at me about the thoughts in my head.

"At least Shay's here," Billy said. "Two Mainers went down too. The younger one was found at the bottom, not far from Shay. They're still looking for the older," He finished, taking a deep sigh.

"It's the first death in what, twenty years, at least?" Mica asked. Billy nodded. Our waters were the roughest, our waves were the biggest, but our surf rescue club was beyond top notch and we always came through for swimmers. But we hadn't today. And that one mistake erased all the years when we'd saved every single swimmer who needed help.

As much as I wanted to cry for the boy who would never return, I was more upset about Shay. She was one of my best friends, and even though she was technically alive, we didn't know why she wasn't responding to anything. And that was scary as hell.

To distract myself from the worst kind of what-ifs sneaking into my brain my thought went to the disaster that was my hair. I knew that I was being shallow, awful, but I couldn't help it. It was better than the alternatives so I went with it.

"Don't yell at me about my thoughts," I said out loud to Mica, too scared and too mad to keep the words inside my brain where they belonged. "I'm not shallow, and my head is usually in the right place. But, I can't help it right now."

"I know," said Billy, soothingly. "It sucks to think about what's going on." He shot a look at Mica and one back at me, and I sensed him reading between the lines. He grew up in a house with Kaleb and Blake, so I wonder if he knew what we could do brain-to-brain. Most people on the island never caught on. Our parents may have suspected but if they did, they chose to ignore it. Their generation firmly believed that if you couldn't see it, it couldn't be real.

But, thought Billy was older than me, he was much younger than them. Still, we'd never talked about with him, and who knew how often Kaleb and Blake had clicked with each other, considering they never really got along too well.

"Just try to relax, Cami. And, Mica, back off," he warned. Mica's huffiness I could handle, but Billy's kindness put me over the edge and I started crying big, ugly sobs.

"Shhh, Cami. It's okay. It's okay," said Billy, taking a break from the buzzing to rub my shoulders. "Just breathe." I leaned into his shoulder and all my worrying gave way to messy tears and mumbled words.

"I should have been paying more attention to her race! I could have gotten to her sooner! She could've been okay," I sobbed.

All our lives, Shayla always, always, had my back and this time—when it mattered most—I hadn't had hers at all. I'd been all about Blake instead.

Watching his race, hugging and kissing him, instead of watching her. That guilt played over again in a loop, that ran from my brain to my heart and back again.

"Cami, between those in competition and those working for the Carnival, there were forty other life guards around."

I looked into Billy's eyes. "But, I didn't even notice right away that something was wrong. When I finally jumped in, we were too late to help. And I still have to get part of my head shaved!" I wailed.

"If you two hadn't gotten to her and brought her up when you did, things would be much, much worse right now. My question is, why didn't anyone else notice?"

"I don't know. I can't even remember what happened," I gasped, attempting to stop the tears. Trying to remember gave me a headache. Mica's antsy energy splintered his thoughts, so they weren't focused enough to help me, either.

"Mica, stop," instructed Billy. "Help me calm Cami down." He put a hand on Mica's shoulder and looked in his eyes. "Or, I will make you leave." Mica stopped pacing and took a deep breath. He pulled a rolling chair up next to mine and grabbed me into a hug. My forehead rested on his shoulder as he held my hair away from the buzzer with one hand and rubbed my back with the other. Privy to his internal struggle to calm himself, I also benefited from his peace when it came.

"Cami, you were with me every second," he said, reassuringly. "And you found her first. If you hadn't told me where she was, then I would have never gone to the right place."

I felt a tiny bit better—until I looked on the floor and saw the huge amount of hair at my feet. "Did you shave my whole head?" I wailed. When I reached up, I realized there was only—and I say 'only' in jest—a large crescent that went from the nape of my neck, up above my right ear. I stroked the soft skin, noting the exposed skin followed the shape of the cut.

In Mica's thoughts, I watched Billy prep a very large needle he planned to place far too close to my brain. I held my breath as I felt the pinch, trying to concentrate on Billy's words as a distraction.

"It's just Lidocaine, Cami; it's going to help the pain, as soon as it kicks in. We'll give it a minute, okay?" He reached into the desk drawer and pulled out three granola bars, the same oat ones in green foil wrappers that we used to eat as little kids.

"What are you? Ten?" Mica asked.

"What can I say? They're good. Amazing how the things you did when you were little still work when you get big." He paused, mussing up his short hair and fixing it again in a way that reminded me of Blake. "Amazing how well you guys managed to communicate mid-rescue," he said in a casual voice that did little to hide the specificity of the topic change.

He looked at me, pursing his lips. "Transmitting information mid-rescue is one of the biggest challenges for The Guard. We have underwater coms, but we don't have time to put them on immediately, or we have to surface to talk. But you guys didn't surface, so how did you let each other know what was going on?"

I raised my head from Mica's shoulder and looked at my twin. I wanted to tell Billy exactly how we'd talked.

Don't tell him. Mica clicked to me. *The Pact.*

A pact we made when we were six? I knew when I felt this strongly about something, the thoughts showed on my face. Billy watched me with an unreadable expression.

Yes. It does. At least ask the others, Mica replied, his emphatic insistence further affecting my anxiety.

"Mica, you're making her…nervous again. What was it?" Billy asked.

"Oh, you know, hand gestures. We spend a lot of time together, just swimming," I said, giggling nervously under Billy's intense stare. "Honestly, it all happened so fast, I barely remember," I said. I closed my eyes, remembering the details and something became clear to me.

"She didn't drown in the typical way," I said, thinking out loud. "It looked like she did a last push underwater."

"That could have seemed strategic—not seen as trouble for such a strong swimmer," Billy said, touching a hand to my head. He touched my head and asked, "Can you feel this?" When I shook my head, he got his needle ready to go.

"She didn't struggle at all on the surface. She dove under on the down stroke of her fly and didn't come back up again." Mica said, nodding in agreement with me.

I felt Mica trying so hard not to watch, but it was sort of like driving by an accident for him; he couldn't keep his eyes from the needle poking through my skin, so I had to witness it, too. Luckily for me, the shot worked, so at least it didn't hurt.

"Hold still, Cam, I'm almost done," said Billy. "So, how did you know to jump in?"

"We just did," we said simultaneously, trading thoughts back and forth like a g-chat when both people write at the same time. I wracked my brain, hoping to see something that could help Billy help Shay without having to give up the biggest secret I shared with my friends.

"The dolphin chatter," I said, "reminded me of First Night. And I was worried, because…"

I paused just as I was about to let it slip that I thought I'd blacked out. While I hadn't said the words out loud, I couldn't reel Mica in.

"You blacked out? You lied about that?" Mica asked out loud. Both my real brother and surrogate brother looked crossly at me.

"I didn't black out," I retorted. "I just don't remember swimming over to the rocks—everything was moving too fast. Just like today. And, you know I didn't black out today," I added, trailing off.

"You were under for a very long time," Billy nodded, finishing his little sewing project on my head. "Perhaps you did run out of breath, but there's really no way to know now. Just to be safe, however, I'm going to run analytics on how long Shayla went without air. It seems, from the incident log, that you guys got to her within three or four minutes of her disappearance. It shouldn't have been long enough to put her in a coma caused by oxygen deprivation. So, if we look at that—and the fact she didn't struggle on the surface—maybe we can learn something new. I'll also check her blood for chemical contamination. Now, Mica, sit down. I need to draw some blood from both of you too."

"We bleed every time we walk into this place," Mica grumbled. "It's like we're some freak science experiment."

I started to argue with Mica, but Billy put a hand on my arm. "Guys, we just need to check that you weren't exposed to anything today that might have something to do with what happened to Shay. This will be over before you know it." Billy had prepped the needle during that sentence and pricked my fingertip while I wasn't looking.

"Ow," I said, more from habit. I'd barely felt a pinch. "You're better at that than Doc is," I said.

"And we would know," Mica said. It was true. We did seem to get blood drawn for every tiny ailment but, in this case, I wasn't going to argue more.

Just let him finish so we can get out of here, I clicked. I just wanted to go and check on Shay and then get home to hide my horrible hair from the world for a bit.

Later that night, I got a text with a "there is no update" update about Shay. Their folks were sending Alysha home and hoped I would go over to keep her company. I arrived to find Alysha sobbing on her sister's bed. For a second, my heart stopped, thinking Shayla was at home and everything was okay again. But my heart couldn't fool my brain for more than a few seconds, because Alysha looked so obviously out of place amongst her twin's things.

The utilitarian locker bed and the swim meet trophies didn't suit Alysha any better than her pink princess room would have suited Shay. Even with mussed make-up, trashed hair and a wrinkly sundress, Alysha was more dressed up than Shay had been at our last Island fundraising gala. I laughed, thinking of the Grecian swim dress Shay had insisted on wearing with gladiator sandals and a high pony, with an outrageous arm cuff that Alysha had made for her. She looked stunning and fierce, and hadn't needed to change for the after-party at the beach—which had been her plan all along.

"Please tell me why you're laughing." Alysha sniffled, making me feel bad.

"I'm sorry, I just—"

"No, I'm not mad," she clarified. "Please tell me, because otherwise I might never laugh again."

I described the memory, and a small giggle escaped her lips, only to be instantly caught by a sob when her own memories mixed in.

"She rated every other dress for utility on a scale of one to ten—especially when that redhead who's always after Blake showed up in that Donna Martin fishtail get-up and fell over. Shay's comments played on a loop inside my head and neither of us could stop laughing at the poor girl," Alysha said. But she quickly stopped laughing at the moment.

Not sure how to react, I let my own giggles fizzle out, dropping onto the bed and snuggling in for a hug. Alysha threw her arms around me and started to sob into my shoulder.

"I can't hear her now," she whispered, so softly.

I released her from the hug to look at her face, hoping against all odds she wasn't really saying what I knew she meant.

"It's like there's a firewall up in her head, stopping me from accessing her."

"I almost told Billy today," I said, chewing on my lip as a few different thoughts appeared, flashing across her face.

"Why?" she asked, eyebrows furrowed in deep thought.

I shook my head. I didn't have an answer. "It seemed like the right thing to me, but Mica stopped me cold. He didn't want anyone wasting time looking at us like freaks when they should be helping Shay," I said. Alysha seemed to buy that reasoning; more than I did, at least.

Alysha and I sat there for what felt like hours, until she'd cried herself out. I cried with her: for Shay, for Alysha, and just the idea that there was anything in the world that could disrupt my twin bond with Mica. Even though it could be really annoying to have him in my head, not having him there would be devastating.

THE NEXT MORNING, I woke up at Shay and Alysha's house. Their parents had not yet come home. My mom was still at the hospital too, so she asked that I remain with Alysha until further notice. I agreed, and managed to cook us some oatmeal, though neither one of us could really eat.

After we were done Alysha insisted on doing my hair to see if she could fix the shaven disaster. She desperately needed an activity to distract her, so I agreed. "It looks…better," she announced after an hour of layering and styling. She'd give me a side ponytail that mostly hid the bandage and the newly exposed skin. I couldn't tell if her excitement level was moderate because of Shayla, or how the hairstyle had turned out; which was, just barely, the right side of okay.

"It looks so much better. Thanks. I just…wish my ears weren't so freakish," I said. I wasn't really happier, but how could I say anything that wasn't at least slightly positive? I felt self-conscious about exposing something I usually kept hidden. Most people complained about big ears, but my tiny ones barely stuck out, leaving my face looking a bit unfinished.

"So your ears are kind of small?" "Who cares? Mine are too," she said, pulling back her blond hair to show me. Her ears were one more example of the very shallow gene pool that stemmed from our families having lived on the Island for so many generations.

"At least you can wear earrings," I said, looking at the little hoops that glittered on her itty-bitty lobes. Mine were even more nonexistent than hers.

"No, you're right, it looks cute and all, but it doesn't look like you." Fluffing, fussing, flipping, the layers fell towards my left shoulder. It exposed the skin, which seemed strange, but actually looked better. "There. That's hot—and fierce—like you," Alysha said, pinning it at the nape of my neck. I agreed, giving a little smile and shaking my head in the mirror. Unfortunately, the sudden movement disturbed the careful arrangement and the mess that resulted left it no better than I'd been after Billy shaved my hair off.

Alysha started to fix it back, but I grabbed her hand.

"Lysh, I love this, and I love you, but you know it will never stay like this."

She nodded and looked through the mirror, straight into my eyes. "Trust me?"

"Of course," I answered, watching her walk out of the bathroom. In a moment, she was back with a black bag that looked disturbingly like the one Billy had at the hospital.

"Oh no, no, no, no!" I said, emphatically, holding my hands over the hair I had left. "No way are you shaving the whole thing off!"

"Cami, I promise, I'm not shaving it off. But I have an idea; the only thing I can think of that'll work," she muttered, taking the clippers out of the bag.

Scrunching my eyes closed, I felt the pulse of the buzzer for the second time, this time over my left ear. Within seconds, I had matching crescents over my ears on both sides of my hair. She stood silently behind while I investigated. "Wow," I said. It looked much better—possibly even better than before my medically-necessitated hair cut. When she gathered it up in a high pony similar to the one Shayla had rocked the night of the benefit, it felt so not frivolous that we had done this. Especially when Alysha slipped on the ear cuff that Shay had worn that night. "So what, if you can't wear earrings? She'd be happy for you to wear this."

I smiled in the mirror and gave Alysha the biggest hug ever. I know it was only a haircut, but our day was a little better than before.

Even though no one had said we could, we went to the hospital, at noon. Alysha felt a desperate need to be with her twin. We'd gone to the hospital with pizza under the premise of bringing everyone lunch, hoping to see Shay.

A new nurse working at the desk screamed upon seeing Alysha. "But, but… you're up," she'd stuttered. "And where did you get those clothes?"

"This is Alysha, Shayla's twin," I murmured, hoping the woman would take a cue from my lower voice, but she didn't.

"People don't look that alike," the woman gasped.

I shook my head and tried to pull my friend away before the nurse could say anything else to make Alysha feel even worse.

The nurse nodded, clearly feeling bad. "I'll pray for Shay," she said, by way of apology, and I nodded thanks and pushed/pulled Alysha down the hallway.

When we got there, Alysha's parents looked drawn, but entirely happy to see their other daughter. They smiled a tiny bit and she dove into their arms. I turned to look around the hallway to give them a little privacy.

"Can I go in?" Alysha asked quietly, turning on a little girl voice that hid the strength she'd shown all night, and this morning, at her house.

Even though we were technically in between visiting hours, my mother, who was there bringing coffee, spoke up on Alysha's behalf.

"Shay's sleeping, essentially, so having Alysha in the room won't hurt her. In fact, it could help," she said, looking at me. "Remember how when they were babies, Cami made it possible for Mica to breathe again? It can only help Shay to have Alysha with her."

He'd come out stillborn and my mom had begged to hold him anyway, and then the two of us together, just

63

once. As soon as I'd landed on her chest next to him, baby Mica had taken a gaspy breath, and a slow heartbeat came back. For the next few days, whenever we were together he would improve, and when we were apart, he'd backslide. Eventually, they just kept us together at all times, just as we'd been in the womb, and within a few weeks he was as healthy as I'd been at birth.

My mom's comment was a really sweet one. We'd barely spoken since my accident, but maybe this could be a little truce.

We stood at the door watching as Alysha laughed, joked, bribed, yelled, negotiated. Anything to get Shay to wake up, but there was no change in her comatose twin. Alysha, however, was much worse off than she'd been when we came in, and her parents didn't do much to make her feel better. They were so worried about Shayla they didn't seem to understand Alysha needed them too.

On my mother's suggestion, we headed out again. Alysha's parents asked me to sleep over and offered a movie night with the boys. I saw Mica and Blake a lot, but hadn't hung out with Darwen and Andrew for days, and I knew they'd be a pick me up for Alysha as well. We went through town, stopping at the grocery for snacks. I made sure to get every one of Alysha's favorites; including the sour gummy worms she loved and I couldn't stand.

Back at her house we had way too much time on our hands. Alysha worked on her jewelry collection, which seemed to help her a bit. There were silver bracelets she was carving words and letters into; mostly song lyrics from what I could tell. I used some of Shayla's gym equipment to get in a light workout. Not swimming didn't mean I had to stop training completely.

"Do some nail art?" I offered, waving my fingers at her.

Her eyes lit up a tiny bit. I'd expected them to. She always begged Shay and me to let her do this to us, but we never said yes. Today, I offered and she made me something that was so adorable I was glad to sit still and watch as she did a tye-dye beach design with a little white dolphin on my pinkie nails.

Just as my nails had dried, the door slammed open. Darwen and Andrew bounced through like puppies, screeching to a halt in front of Alysha and calming down to give her a hug.

"Sorry about Shay," Andrew said.

Darwen gave the best hugs. It was his superpower. I watched her relax into his strong arms and felt so grateful her parents were letting the others come over because this was exactly what we all needed. All the twins born our year had a special bond. There were two more, Hale and Leah. They'd moved away when we were kids. I hardly remembered them but I still missed having them there.

Like Kaleb, there was a sense that we all belonged together. Their lack of presence was a vague ache. Kaleb's absence was still a sharp pain. And Shayla's, well the pain from missing her was sliced open, raw, and bleeding. It had only been a day. But with each hour it felt worse, instead of better.

Andrew and Darwen were identical twins, but not mirrors of one another. This was a critical difference, at least as much as they compared to Kaleb and Blake. They were best friends, attached at the hip, partners in crime who played constant tricks on me; the way people always imagined twins did. They looked exactly alike in every way except for their hair; Darwen's was flat and Andrew had a little cowlick. Luckily, this held true even when they were wet.

They were fun, never taking anything too seriously. Very quickly, they dragged us both into a game of spoons. Ridiculously simple, we passed around cards trying to get four of a kind and when we did we grabbed one of the spoons in the middle of the table. Everyone else followed, but with one less spoon, someone got locked out each time. It was mindless, yet somehow exciting, and stupidly competitive. So much so, I jammed my finger into the table and bent the nail back.

"Ouch!" I said, looking pissed at my ruined nail polish.

Alysha's eyes went big. "Since when do you care about your nails?"

"Since I let you spend two hours on them. Besides, that hurt," I said, pouting at Andrew.

"Says the girl who didn't feel a cut requiring sixteen stitches?" Mica asked, walking through the door. He came over and tugged my ponytail gently. "Who knew the hospital had a beauty shop?"

As I jumped to defend Alysha and myself, he stopped me. "Teasing, Cami. Just kidding. Looks good, actually," he said, turning to Alysha. "Want to do mine, too?"

Minutes later, Mica walked back in the room.

"Like it?" he asked, shaking his head in my face to show off the change in his hairline.

His hair was dark with tons of gold highlights, just like mine was, but much shorter at the moment. I nodded and even smiled a bit, seeing in his head how much it looked like the back of mine, minus the ponytail, of course. I felt an incredible amount of comfort from that.

"They look like wings," Blake said, walking in from the kitchen, carrying a huge bowl of ice cream with spoons for all.

My heart jumped to see him, especially at the small smile he shot my way. He placed the ice cream on the coffee table. Still conditioned from our earlier game, I reached out super-fast and grabbed the closest spoon. Everybody laughed.

Heaped with Alysha's favorite mint chocolate ice cream, I handed it over, hoping this would entice her to eat. She'd put nothing in her stomach since breakfast. While I could certainly understand her lack of an appetite for the pizza at the hospital, I still worried about her.

"Or fins, I think. Angel fins," I said, thinking about the way Blake had looked when he came out of the water to rescue me the other night.

"What are angel fins?" Andrew asked, laughing.

I shrugged, looking around the room. It felt almost normal, except for missing Shay, which preyed on my mind.

"Um, you guys?" I asked, tentatively. It seemed wrong, what I needed to ask of them, but it felt right. Mica gave me a look, began to open his mouth, but I silenced him with one of my own. All eyes in the room (all shades of silver, except for Blake's mismatched pair) found me. "I want to tell Billy and Celeste about our twin links. Maybe it could help Shay," I said, forcing the words out nervously without taking a breath.

"What? That I can't hear her in my head anymore? They'll think I'm crazy," Alysha's eyes went teary as she threw the question at me.

She began shaking her head quickly. Andrew put an arm around her in a sideways hug, watching me warily, while Darwen crossed his arms and shook his head vehemently. "They'll just do freaky tests on her. On Shay."

"On all of us," Darwen said angrily. "Those guys at the Ocean Research Institute will turn us into guinea pigs…"

"Again," Andrew finished, a little more gently.

"Celeste is at the Institute, she won't let them hurt us," I said, looking at Blake for support. He nodded at me, but still looked unsure.

"They should be doing lots of tests on Shayla, anyway," Mica said. They'd put Shay's incident down to a freak accident, and everyone seemed to be accepting that, at least according to our mom. "How can it be a random accident when those other boys also went down?" Mica asked angrily. He was frustrated that they weren't looking into the connection between the two incidents.

"I don't want them to hurt her, or any of us," Alysha said, stubbornly. "Besides, it's only been a day. What if she wakes up tomorrow, and then she'll be pissed, because we'll be treated like freaks for no reason. No, we should stick to the pact. She'd want it that way."

Five heads nodded around the room in agreement, but the idea hung on my brain and wouldn't let go. I tried one more thing.

"What about us telling only Billy? He lived with you and…" I trailed off, not mentioning Kaleb by name. No one did. It was one of those things. Blake was the Island golden boy, sort of our Harry Potter, which made Kaleb He-Who-Must-Not-Be-Named. Though I didn't think he was evil, the others definitely seemed to. Blake's strong, usually open features were set like a statue, emotionless. He paused, clearly being careful to consider any words he uttered about his twin.

"We never quite enjoyed the connection the way you all do. I don't think Billy ever suspected anything," Blake said evenly. But I knew he'd chosen his words with care. They had the link but they didn't like it.

It had caused so many fights that I felt certain Billy knew Before Kaleb and Blake started arguing about every single thing, we even used to joke and do contests with the twin link thing. We'd made a pact to stop talking about it. But I'd always assumed Kaleb and Blake had kept doing it, just as the rest of us did.

"Okay," I agreed. "We won't say anything. Who wants ice cream?" I said, reaching for a spoon, but more gently this time than during the game.

"Pistachio is on the other side," Blake pointed, grabbing a spoon and loading it with my favorite flavor and passing it my way. Our fingers brushed when I took it from him, thanking him with my eyes and sliding the treat slowly into my mouth as he watched. I couldn't help but remember how our shared marshmallow had transformed into a kiss, and wondered if the ice cream could, too. From the way Blake licked his lips as he watched, he may have wondered as well.

It seemed frivolous to think such things after the tough conversation we'd just had, but I wanted to let go for a few minutes. He ran his hand over his hair from back to front and looked at me. There was definitely something new in the way he looked at me, a heat that flowed between us that had not existed before First Night. I couldn't ignore it, or push it off as a tension breaker. The energy reached me, pulling my brain back to that kiss on the beach and made me nod, and go towards him, even before he said the words. "I want the fin wings too, but I want Cami to do it."

Alysha's eyes widened, then crinkled up at the corners, as she attempted to hide a smile. I didn't know if she felt guilty smiling with Shay in a coma, or if she was trying to play it cool for me. Either way, I felt grateful for her subtlety when Andrew, Darwen, and Mica started nudging each other and making funny faces at Blake and me.

"Ignore them," Alysha said, laughing, "but go on the porch. I'm tired of cleaning up hair in the bathroom."

"Will you buzz it all over for me, before you make the wing things?" Blake asked. "It's a little too long anyway."

"What number?" I asked, staring at his shoulders, the pulse in his neck. He squirmed, trying to get adjusted, attempting to move close enough between his legs so I could get the job done. I had to stretch my legs open just to fit, and his broad back immediately filled in every space that I made available.

I warned myself not to overthink anything, to just enjoy the feelings that flowed. This was case positive proof that something had changed. Because I'd done this before and it had truly just been about hair. This was all about Blake. And me.

He sat up straight on the bench, between my legs, while I sat on top of the picnic table on Alysha's deck. I was glad she'd sent us out here, even with the teasing. The bathroom would have been all kinds of too small for Blake's six-foot plus form and my new attraction to it. I starved for fresh air because staring at him like this had taken my breath away.

Carefully keeping an inch between us, I studied the settings on the buzzer and tried to stop the intense shaking in my hands.

"Two all over, and zero on the wings," he said leaning back and closing the distance between us.

His neck came to the top of my thigh as he tilted back his head to stare at me upside down. I ran my hand through the hair over his forehead, considering where to start.

His hair was thick, soft, and rough all at the same time. My fingers rubbed down to the scalp and over to his right ear. With the buzzer at his temple, I pressed down firmly and used my hand to clear a line around the spiral shell of his ear that looked just like Alysha's and mine, Blake appeared to share the same small-ear gene. In eighteen years, I'd never noticed ears as much as I had today.

"Starting with the wings, huh?" he asked, smiling into my eyes and breaking into my thoughts.

All my attention shifted to him. "I uh, just thought I might do a better job this way," I stuttered, switching to the left side and cutting carefully, so that the two sides would match. With that done, I pushed his head back straight so I could reach the hair in the back.

"Yeah, well that's good. Remember when you did this for the all-city swim meet? Because you kinda sucked at it then," he said, reaching up a long arm to bop me on the head.

He and Mica had asked me to buzz their hair before a particularly competitive swim meet. Seeking every advantage, they went for zero on the clippers, meaning close to clean-shaven bald. Blake went first. Halfway through, I'd pressed down too hard and drawn blood. In his usual chivalrous fashion, he'd ignored his own pain to calm me down after I'd made him bleed.

"Stay still!" I grabbed his skull, holding on tightly to make sure he didn't move. "I don't want to cut you."

"Again," he grimaced.

"Nope, we've had enough head injuries already this week," I said.

"Shay's was a head injury?" he asked.

"No, I mean me," I said nervously. Bringing up that night I'd gotten hurt brought up the kisses too, at least in my mind.

"All right, then two minor head injuries isn't really so bad," he said, diffusing all of my guilt with an easy smile and a casual rub on my knee.

The night I'd cut him, he'd given me far more hugs than I'd been comfortable with, and bought me ice cream.

That knock to my head on First Night splintered the pieces of my friendship with Blake like a kaleidoscope. The moments hadn't changed, the way I saw them had. The new arrangement highlighted memories and images in a new formation, and I suddenly understood that Celeste had been right. Some part of Blake had been thinking about me, about us for a while now. I was just now catching up.

I wanted to ask. It would have been easy with him trapped, facing away from my eyes. But I lost my nerve when he opened his mouth to speak instead.

"Don't leave any rooster spots. You know, all those little patches you left sticking up all over last time?" he said, reaching up to swat away some bits of hair stuck to his eyelashes.

"Better rooster than bald eagle," I said. "Now, stay still." I pushed his arm down against his side and pressed my legs around him, clamping him between my knees to finish up the last few rows.

Blake crossed his arms, giving in, as I completed the second-to-last row. "I can still move," he said, using his right hand to tickle my left ankle. My foot kicked out, a reflex action that threw my clippers off-path. A partially shaved patch of hair stuck up right in the middle of his head.

"Okay, fine, I'm done, then," I said. I turned the buzzer off and started to stand.

Blake wrapped one arm under my leg to keep me from getting up and used the other to feel around his head, stopping right at the rough spot. He trapped my other leg and we were back in the same position as before. He was sitting between my legs, but now he had immobilized me.

"Pick up the clippers, Cami."

"Can't make me," I said, giggling.

"Calliope Camille, pick up the clippers, or we'll be here all night."

That wouldn't be so bad, I thought, though I didn't say it out loud. With enough time, I could gather up the bravery I'd need to kiss him again. We sat stalemated, for a moment, as I considered my next move. Chickening out on the kiss, I picked up the clippers and finished buzzing the spot.

"Done," I said. But, he still didn't release my legs.

"Check it?" he asked.

I felt all around, from the front to the back, and all the way up again, paying special attention to the completely bared spots on the sides. The crescents that looked so much like mine felt smooth and hot under my thumbs. I stroked those same spots over and over again, thinking about Shay.

"I want her to get better, too," he whispered, grabbing my hand. "But, I did this for you." He ran his finger along the inside, drawing a spiral on my skin. He went around in the small circle a few times and on every loop I felt the temperature climb higher on my skin.

That's when I felt the clicks. Buzzing from brain, to bone, to blood, they told me exactly what to do. Seconds slowed and movement stilled until only the magnetic pull between us existed. Upside down and backwards, perfect. I kissed his forehead, then his nose and then moved down. The awkwardness of the angle disappeared as soon as his mouth met mine, giving way to the bliss that bloomed on my lips and blasted all through me. With that I no longer minded my hair, because it had brought this second connection to Blake. And if it meant he kept kissing me like this, I could deal.

five

I GOT TO stay on beach patrol as Doc had promised. But I wasn't allowed on the beach. The next day I landed pool duty, and since I wasn't allowed to get in and get my head wet, I had to spend all day in the baby zone. A definite downgrade from the beach, but at least it got me outside. Alysha spent the day at the hospital with Shay, and I hoped to be able to visit that night.

The town pool was a Pinhold institution. It was where we'd spent our summers until the age of ten, when we started in the Junior Guard. The rhythm of the day was always the same; a forty-five minute free swim followed by fifteen minutes of adult swim every hour, except for noon, when the adults got the pool for sixty whole minutes. Adult swim meant intense games of wall ball or kickball on the playground throughout the day. It had been years since I'd really spent all day like this, and I felt pleased none of it had really changed.

Celeste came for the noon swim. She took one look at my face and instead of swimming, dragged me to the beach for my lunch break. "Greasy food, gorgeous waves, and a little girl-talk to put things in perspective," she said. She sighed and looked at me like she could see right through me. "No, Cami, I haven't asked Blake about you," she said unprompted, shaking her head at me in a way that made her seem way older than her twenty-four years. "And, I don't need to. If you want him, he's definitely gonna want you, too. That's how it works. You just don't know it yet."

At that moment, a seagull swept down and snagged a French fry right out of Celeste's hand, flying back to the railing and chomping it slowly with a satisfied look. Celeste and I laughed so hard that the little guy looked embarrassed. Of course, I had to feed him another fry to make up for laughing at him. This time, he took it from my hand and flew with it under the boardwalk to enjoy it—away from our prying eyes. As the seagull cawed its thanks, I thought of another time a seagull ate my French fry, three years and forever ago, and sighed.

"Kaleb always said he felt about as wanted on this Island as a seagull at a picnic," I said, letting my thoughts drift. His presence was still everywhere even though he'd managed to steer clear of Pinhold for years.

"Wow, you're the first person to ever mention his name without major prying on my part," commented Celeste. "It seems like everything I know about that kid I've found out online." I nodded, knowing she was right. But my lunch break was limited, and I didn't want to spend it talking about the wrong brother. "Okay, fine," she said, rolling her eyes when I went silent. "No Kaleb questions for you, either. But, don't worry about Blake. He definitely likes you. Haven't your parents been planning your marriage since birth?" She laughed, but I wasn't laughing with her. "Seriously, that picture of you guys naked and kissing on your grandmother's porch swing? It would make the perfect wedding invitation."

"Yeah, sure—but that picture wasn't me and Blake."

"No? But I thought he was the one everyone wanted for you."

I nodded. He was. "He's the golden boy. Kaleb's the black sheep. Maybe I was drawn to him because he needed me more."

"And because choosing him was sort of an F.U. to what they wanted for you, don't you think?"

"I didn't choose him. I didn't choose anyone. We were little kids, just friends."

Celeste nodded just a little too knowingly for me to feel comfortable. "I wonder if you saw him now, how you both would react."

I grumbled under my breath and got up to toss my trash. I didn't really need to think about that. Kaleb wasn't here, and Blake and I seemed like we were starting something that I really liked. Maybe it wasn't a big deal, or maybe he would be the love of my life. I had no idea yet. But the one thing I did know what that if I kept thinking about Kaleb, I'd wreck everything before it began.

When Celeste and I got back to the pool, minutes later, Blake had taken over one of the lap lanes for practice. I got to watch each muscle of his eight-pack flex each time he pistoned his hips above the surface, which— thankfully—he did over and over again. As a swimmer, I understood that the upward thrust was necessary to build muscle memory. As his maybe-because-we-hadn't-talked- about-it girlfriend, the only thing I understood was that watching him pulse his body over and over again made me think very R-rated thoughts that had no place at the baby pool!

Celeste came over, after she finished her own laps, teasing me so my face turned red. "All those women are judging your boy," she said, pointing to a row of moms who looked about ready to hold up numbers like Olympic judges. It was almost obnoxious, though I understood the captivation.

"They should just stop it, already. It doesn't get more perfect-10 than that," I said, sighing and shaking my head. I had watched Blake swim millions of strokes and it had never turned me on at all.

"Nah," she grinned wickedly. "He loses a point for wearing clothes."

I shushed her, because he was heading my way, but he surprised both of us by jumping back in the pool. I watched as he swam over to the ladder and helped the elderly Mr. Pollack up the steps and into his wheel chair. That earned him a kiss from Mrs. Pollack, who usually did the job herself, with a strength that was at odds with her age.

"All right," Celeste grumbled, "if he's gonna be that sweet, he can have the extra point."

I nodded, glad she agreed. Not that it mattered what she thought about Blake. I was more worried about what he thought about me.

I spent the rest of the day watching the pool in silence, grateful the whistle could speak the most basic commands for me. Blake asked me to wait to take my dinner break until after he finished hauling in beach chairs for The

Guard. I blew the "all clear" whistle after the 6:00PM adult swim when his deep laugh pulled me out of the fugue state, brought on by a whole day of baby pool non-activity.

"Heard you got the new record for the kiddie fly! Way to go, Maisy!" Blake said. I shifted my eyes to the entrance in time to see Blake catch the six-year-old in the air and spin her around. He was great with little kids—just like Billy had been with us.

"I taught her everything I know," purred Maisy's redheaded mom Stella, slowly peeling herself off of a lounge chair like a not-so-stealth cougar. Even with years of practice, I could never pull off that move—which was why I found it so disturbing that it caught Blake's attention.

He put Maisy down gently and stuttered a quick 'Hi' to the fake-boobed female who stalked over to him. Watching him struggle to look at anything besides her chest would have been hilarious if I wasn't instantly so jealous. It felt icky.

The ten minutes until my break seemed like an incredibly long opportunity for Stella to sink in her claws. I didn't want to gift her with that much time to cause drama in my life. The baby pool was empty, so I jumped in with a loud splash and started playing pool-toy basketball with the boats and buckets floating around. As diversions went, it did the trick.

Blake saw me and grabbed the opportunity to break away to help. I tried not to read too much into how quickly he covered the ground over to where I was. He was rushing away from Stella, but I'd take it!

He picked up the bucket that held the toys, moving it over, so I had to work a little harder to sink the shots. Though she was six—and technically too big for the baby pool—Maisy followed him over and got in on the game. When the clean-up was done too soon for her, she jumped out, grabbed the bucket, and dumped all thirty toys back into the pool. I groaned as Blake laughed.

"Maisy, you just gave Cami here a lesson in Karma."

"Caramel?" the little girl asked, hopefully.

"No, not caramel. Karma. It's when the things you do come back to you," Blake said patiently, tossing a fully dimpled grin right at me. "We used to do the exact same thing to my brother and your mommy at least five times a day when they were lifeguards at the pool."

I remembered and laughed with Blake.

"Got it," she shrugged, looking around his back. "Do you have any candy? You could pay me for my help?" Blake smiled, admitting defeat. He reached in his bag, passing Maisy a chocolate-covered pretzel.

"Go ask your mommy if you can eat this," he said, sending the little girl on her way.

"And you," he said, pointing to me, "ready for dinner? I brought a picnic for the beach."

Once we got onto the sand, Blake pulled a red-and-white checked blanket out of his pack to lay out by the water. He came prepared—which made me squeal silently to myself.

"Is there a chocolate-covered pretzel in there for me too?" I asked, digging in the bag. We were on 'my' rock, a little corner of the jetty where I used to come to fish with my dad. It had little tally marks where we had scratched a line for each fish we had caught over the years.

It wasn't the best fishing spot—we could catch more right outside our house—so there were only fourteen lines. But my dad liked it best because, he swore you could hear the currents meet. I could never quite understand what he meant, but I liked to watch the waters come together, swirl, and separate. And, I could be alone in the very center of the action. Since only people fishing were allowed on the rocks, I kept an old pole hidden in a crevice. I would put it up beside me, securing a little solitude even on the busiest beach days.

I went to bite into the pretzel, but Blake grabbed it out of my hand. "Protein first," he said, touching my hand for a bit longer than necessary, replacing the pretzel with dark chocolate almond bark.

"Thanks for the sugar," I said. "But, what makes it dinner?"

Blake's eyes grew wide in disbelief. "How could you not remember Barf Night?"

Oh. My. God. Blake had replicated the menu from the single-most-humiliating-night-of-my-life.

We were thirteen and Kaleb had just left, and our parents had agreed to let us go to the boardwalk by ourselves for the first time. It was a short ferry ride away on the mainland, which was a big deal at the time. But then, Mica had gotten the flu, and I was crushed, thinking we wouldn't get to go at all. Blake convinced my dad that he and I could go it alone. He promised to protect me and hold my hand the entire time. So, that's what we did.

"Could you please forget that night ever happened?" I begged. Blake moved over, nudging me with his shoulder. I jumped when his arm touched mine.

"Cami, I had more fun that night than I'd ever had on the boardwalk—barf and all."

Thinking back on that night, I had felt so full of energy from the rush of freedom and the zip from the rides. We used half the money we'd brought on wristbands that allowed us unlimited rides, pooling all our other funds for a candy-store bonanza that would have never been permitted had our parents been around. The huge sugar surge overloaded my system and did me in—resulting in the incredibly disgusting ending. We had to call Billy to come pick us up, so we didn't have to ride the boat home with my barf covering us both.

"It wasn't all bad," I admitted. "You were pretty cool about the whole thing. You even kept holding my hand after I puked on you."

Blake laughed. "Billy teased the hell out of me for that," he said. "For years . . ." Funny—Billy had teased me about everything else under the sun, as long as I'd known him, but he'd never mentioned that night to me. Confused, I looked up to see a great big smile on Blake's face. "He's the one who called it 'Barf Night'. Even his college roommate knows the story: 'How Blake got puked on the first time he managed to go anywhere alone with a girl,'" he said, mocking himself. "I know you're bummed about missing the Surf Carnival and Shay, so I figured this might cheer you up," he said, smiling at me. "I've always remembered it as a really great night."

The kaleidoscope had turned again. Far from horrible, that night had meant so much to him. More, even, then he'd put into words yet. I could see him wavering, wondering how much to tell me, what might draw me in, or scare me away.

A few days ago, any bit of it would have sent me running for the cliffs. But with Shay in the hospital, I had a sudden and terrible reminder that life wasn't guaranteed. Days didn't belong to us until we'd lived in them and passed them into memories. Did I really want to pass this present, this beautiful boy working so hard to charm me? Did I dare from him for wanting to pull me in closer to this life, all for the sake of a future that might never be mine?

Lit by the sun shimmering on the waves, I finally heard the currents smack together. Time stopped for just a second to tell me that what was happening with me and Blake was absolutely meant to be. My breath caught again as I looked up at him. I leaned in as his eyes widened and his lips parted.

Every bone in my body, every wave on the rocks, and every bird in the sky screamed for me to kiss him. His eyes closed, and he moved toward me. His hand moved from my shoulder and up my neck, right under my hair.

It tickled and I lost my nerve. As the giggles rose and my face turned red, I buried my face in his shirt. The ocean picked that exact minute to smack us in the face with a big wave. I jumped back and squealed, wet from the wave. It was the perfect excuse to scoot closer to Blake. When I closed my eyes and raised my lips, he took the hint and kissed me.

Each time our lips met, my brain blocked everything else out. I heard the sound of the ocean, but only because the waves beat to the rhythm of the truth pounding in my ears that told me over and over again this felt so absolutely, incredibly, inexplicably right.

six

I HAD ALMOST complete inventory of lifeguarding equipment in The Guard's beach headquarters when I heard them call my grandfather down to the beach over the short-wave radio that stayed on all day. That thing had been giving me a headache while I worked, and I'd actually been about to turn it down when the call came in. about multiple dolphins stranding. I locked the door to headquarters and ran to get there at the same time as Gramps, offering to help in any way I could.

Dolphin cries filled the air as they had during First Night when so many of them had breeched on the shore. This situation was different because, a mother and calf had washed up together and the baby had died. The mother knew, and was suffering. We attempted to remove the body, but the mother moved so violently on the sand that we stopped. She only calmed down when the little one was placed against her stomach.

At five-hundred pounds, the mother couldn't be moved without help from the tides or professional rescue equipment. Unfortunately, everything we had was tied up with a mass stranding event twenty miles up the coast where the dolphins had been turning up beached in record numbers, for days. They were only able to save half, if that many.

The numbers were so high this year all over California for strandings and deaths, that these ones today didn't have a chance for professional attention. But Gramps knew what to do; having helped for so many years before the Institute even existed. The dolphin's sounds had quieted, though it seemed more like cries than the usual clicks and whistles heard in the water. I wanted to cry too, but I kept it together because there were so many little kids around, trying to help.

Four hours later, we were trying to keep the poor thing cool and covered enough, hoping we could keep going until the tide came in enough to get her out to sea. She whimpered quietly, while her breathing grew louder. I sang one of the sea chants my grandfather had taught me long ago. He joined along, his gruff voice catching on the exact notes and tones that sounded like the ocean.

I concentrated on the tune and rubbing the dolphin's head, while Gramps gently poured water on the special sailcloth covering her and keeping her skin moist. Two dolphins had used this cloth over a hundred years ago, to save an ancestor of mine from drowning when his boat got destroyed in a storm. They'd carried him back to shore on the sheet; it had been precious to our family ever since.

I hoped its luck wouldn't fade today. Over and over, I traced a swirl pattern on her head. She seemed to stay quiet as long as I was touching her.

"I can do the water," I said, switching spots with my grandfather. He sat and I stood. Almost immediately, the dolphin cried.

Gramps shook his head. "I will take care of the water, Cami. What you're doing is much more important."

I sat, going back to the pattern I traced on the top of her head. I didn't know why it helped, but I felt grateful it did.

"Did you realize that you are making The Swirl over the spot between her eyes—the Sacred Swirl? The Sacred Swirl represents protection—like the shape of our island," he said.

"Or a sea shell?" I asked.

"Exactly," he said.

"Ears?" I wondered, putting a self-conscious hand to those that had been so newly exposed by my short hair.

He nodded and smiled at me. "If you look, you'll find it everywhere," he said, stroking the same pattern over her large flank under the cloth.

It seemed to calm her. I'd never considered it had any specific symbolism; I just knew it comforted me.

"That's why mothers do the same thing to babies before they fall asleep," he said.

I wrinkled my eyes, thinking back. "Did my mother ever do it to Mica and me?" I asked.

"No," he said, "but the rest of us did, your dad, Grams, and me."

I nodded, imagining my mother dismissing the idea that symbolic touches would help anything. I wondered if she'd done it for any of the babies who'd died in the years the Islanders had struggled with interrupted fertility. I looked in the sad eyes of the dolphin, understanding more about losing a baby from her gaze than from anything my mother had ever said.

Sacred swirl, or luck of the tide, or both, we had the dolphin back in the water two hours later. My grandfather and three of The Guard dragged her out to sea on the sailcloth, with the baby beside her. The high tide meant the Island's famous water organ was in harmony with the ocean and the waves. It added an element of hope, in the way music often did.

In the ocean, I saw Gramps and The Guard pulling the sailcloth away as the dolphin wiggled into the water. The baby remained on the white shroud until two other dolphins came over, and only then did Gramps release the body into the sea. The new dolphins worked together to keep it on the surface of the water, and pushed it between them, swimming with it while also leading the mother to the pod deeper out to sea. It looked like a funeral, and I watched tearfully even when they were too far for me to see them anymore.

THAT NIGHT, AT the hospital, I got some alone time with Shay while Blake and Alysha went for coffee. During our few minutes of quiet, I held Shay's hand, making the sacred swirl in her palm and wishing like mad it would help her— as it had helped the dolphin earlier. It felt to me like she was in there—but maybe that was wishful thinking.

After my conversation with my grandfather, I'd started noticing the Sacred Swirl design everywhere. I found swirled shells all over the beach—so often it seemed like they were finding me. I brought some for Shay to keep by her bed, even though it seemed like protecting her might be moot.

A blast of air blew into the room from a door opening and closing further down the hallway. A wisp of Shay's hair blew onto her forehead, which would have driven her crazy had she been awake. Brushing her hair back behind her ear, I noticed the Sacred Swirl in her ear. Her ears were so small and delicate for someone of her size and strength; just like my own.

A student-nurse came in and quietly made notes on a chart, and I studied her as she worked. Pale, with brown eyes and brown hair, she looked nothing like those of us who lived on-Island. An old-fashioned looking white cap sat on top of her head, making her ears stick out in a way that was most obvious. The Sacred Swirl was visible there, but it was stretched out and not as balanced as it seemed on Shay.

When Alysha and Blake walked in the room, I started talking quickly about Shay's ears, how mine and Shay's were so alike, but the nurses were different. They shared a look; concern that I'd lost it

"What does this have to do with anything?" Blake asked, looking at me.

"Who else has this?" Alysha asked.

"Well, just us, and when the nurse came into the room and her ears were completely different, it made me think," I said. "Why do we all have the same ears? And, what if that has something to do with what's happened to Shay? Or..."

"Calm down, ok? Take a deep breath," Blake said, putting a finger to my lips. "Before you go all Mica on us and jump to a zillion conclusions, let try to see if you're on to something here." He texted Billy who agreed to come by the hospital to see if there was anything unusual about Shay's ears.

I inhaled deeply and nodded. I was worried if there was something to this, what happened to her could happen to us.

seven

"GONNA BE A little hard to call this a coincidence now," Mica said, pacing so fast the ancient boards creaked louder than the water.

Only a week later, Darwen had an accident like Shay's. He was in a coma too.

The last bits of burnished red faded over the bay, bringing in all the sounds of night on the water. I sat with my legs dangling off the dock, steeling myself against the slight chill in the air that was so unusual for this time of year, but seemed so appropriate given the mood. Mica built a fire in the bowl on the deck for the two of us, and the snap and crackle sounded slow and lazy, like it was missing energy. I felt the same way.

Cool winds blew the reeds on the river dunes, whistling and whooshing, making them sound alive. Off in the distance, I heard the call of the dolphins. They sounded sad tonight, but maybe that was just me projecting my feelings onto them. I desperately wanted to go for a swim to clear my head, and with my stitches finally out I'd finally been given the all-clear to get wet, but the beach was closed for the day.

I chimed in, "The Guard will have to get more involved now that Darwen…" But I stopped, because I was feeding

Mica's anger, which upset me even more. I couldn't take on his feelings. I had far too many of my own to process. Luckily, he took the hint and went inside the house, taking his anger with him. Yesterday, they'd finally found the body of the boy who went missing at the Ocean Swim. He had turned up in the middle of the main beach with ten dead dolphins.

We hadn't had an accidental death from drowning on Pinhold in over twenty years. It was only the beginning of July and we'd already had two. It called our commitment and our abilities, into question. While the boys' deaths were labeled accidents, they'd happened during competition. So there was talk from the state about changing Surf Carnival regulations, which may have made sense but offended everybody here.

What no one wondered, at least out loud, was if Shay's coma was somehow related to the death of the boys. Since she was technically still alive, her case hadn't really been studied by anyone but local doctors. Mica seemed convinced there was a link, which Doc knew, and he was hiding something.

I was sure he was wrong, until today, when Darwen nearly drowned as well. He was in the hospital bed next to Shay and it seemed impossible to think all these events were completely random, considering it all happened in one ocean, in our small part of the world. I'd been in the office getting my stitches out when word came in. I'd asked, casually if it was the same thing that had happened to Shay, and Doc had dismissed the notion so fast I wondered if he'd even heard me. So, I repeated it again and realized he was deliberately ignoring me.

According to the onlookers who had notified The Guard, Darwen had disappeared from the surface and hadn't come up again. Like Shay, he went down without the usual physiological signs of drowning. He simply disappeared below the surface of the ocean.

Because it was dusk, no one had noticed, immediately. In fact, the Guard had a very difficult time locating him. They searched for at least half an hour before his location was identified by a pod of dolphins, keening sadly, like they had lost one of their own.

While they weren't using words, I knew they were talking out their pain. I so badly wanted to join them in the water so I could do the same. I felt a yearning to see the white dolphin from the other night. After my rescue, she felt special to me, and I'd been more relieved than was right when her body wasn't one of those found lifeless on the beach. Feeling connected to a specific dolphin wasn't unheard of on Pinhold—that's how it used to be when there were more dolphins than people.

Old Island legends said everyone who lived here had their own dolphin twin who guarded the sea, as we guarded the land. But, after the oil spill in the 1960s, that changed. By the time my mom was born, the dolphin population had dwindled so dramatically most of the people never swam with dolphins, much less found their dolphin twin. That broke the connection for so many people my mom's age that they didn't seem to have any spiritual relationship with the ocean or the dolphins. Those who still lived here focused on the tangible, visible elements of Pinhold life. The rest left the Island entirely.

I never counted on having a dolphin twin, but it was beginning to feel like I did, when I suddenly spotted the albino who had rescued me with her pod not far from the dock at my house, right in front of me.

She swam up, skin shining in the dimming light. A fresh scar by her eye was more pronounced than the others dotting her otherwise smooth back and I knew she'd gotten it saving me.

Circling the reeds, her clicks and whistles called to me. She somehow made sense to me on a day when not much else did.

I dove in head first, approaching her slowly as I came up for air. My entire body seemed to sigh with the relief from being back in the water, as well as the proximity to my dolphin. Close up, her skin had a sheen I hadn't noticed before. It almost seemed iridescent and I couldn't resist reaching out. She turned her head to me, intentionally or not, giving me a clear view of the multiple raised bumps that made up her latest scar. Lots of small cuts appeared as dots close up. Together they made a swirled crescent that almost looked like a tattoo.

Her huge silver eye stared into mine, and it felt like I was looking into a mirror; the color the same as mine. She nodded her head and dove underwater. Like I had done on First Night, I followed her.

She held back speed as we made our way through the reeds, rocking her fluke casually through the water. At first, I struggled with a traditional breaststroke, arms spreading out and legs following behind. Slowly, though, I changed the position of my legs, keeping them together and mimicking the movement of her body. Soon, I needed my arms only for navigation, or an occasional burst of speed. They worked to propel me from the water, whenever I needed air.

Quickly, we joined her pod of five, and I swam faster than I ever had in my life in order to keep up. I found myself hundreds of yards from home, in the dark, out of breath. I stilled, treaded water, and panicked.

My heart sounded louder than the waves, crashing way too far away on the shore. The lighthouse, partially dimmed by a layer of fog, stood in the distance, and—thinking of the dangers to Shay and to Darwen—the tears I'd held in all day burst like a hurricane-ruined dam.

The white dolphin called out and the others came back and circled me, so quickly the water around me became like a whirlpool, and I had to fight to keep from slipping down. Her friends went away, leaving she and I alone. She circled me, calming me until my panic subsided, and led me back toward my house where I saw a figure waiting for me in the shallows.

It was Blake, and I recognized him not as my best-friend-turned-boyfriend, but as another being belonging to the sea.

There was a dolphin there with him, in the marsh, and we all stared at each other.

"Cami! You're okay?" Blake asked from where he treaded water.

"Better than," I chirped, the excitement in my voice sounding much like the dolphins on their happy days. My dolphin seemed to smile at me, and I watched Blake's eyes go wide as the dolphin he swam near did the same thing.

I giggled at their similar expressions, which seemed to break the odd tension of the situation. Reassured I wasn't in danger, Blake relaxed as much as anyone could when swimming less than ten feet from an eight-foot long, five-hundred pound creature.

"I'm glad to hear you happy," Blake said, appreciation for my changed mood all over his face. The moonlight glinted off his teeth, exaggerating his smile, and the dolphin flashed his teeth as well; all twenty rows!

Blake and the male dolphin traded megawatt smiles back and forth, making me laugh so hard I snorted. My girl shook her head at the noise, like she was surprised, and the movement rippled through the water, splashing me and making me snort water out of my nose.

That became the new game: splash the human to see if it would make the snorting noise again. Over and over, they experimented with us, and even successfully imitated the sound. While we were all highly amused, the extra splashing made me cold, and treading water wasn't enough to warm me up again. It was time to go in.

The dolphins stayed by us until we were safely on the dock Then they turned around, ducked under water, came back out, and snorted through their blowholes, as if saying goodbye. I realized that, while nothing changed in my world outside the water, they had completely changed my perspective.

Popping wood and crackling sparks filled the silence as Blake and I sat on a bench together, borrowing heat from the fire Mica had built just a few hours earlier. When I shivered, he pulled me closer, threading my legs through his. This comforting cuddle was completely new—scary and right at the same time, the way everything with Blake had become lately.

The curling smoke shifted, turning directions a split second before I felt the wind change on my skin. The pounding waves slowed as the chatter of the dolphins quickened. They were far off in the distance, but somehow I felt like they were still connected to me—to both of us. And they were definitely cheering me on.

I felt every hour of swim practice in those muscles that suddenly pressed against mine. I never knew I had so many nerve-endings going up and down my side, but I felt all kinds of buzzing in places that never seemed all that important before. And then, his fingers started moving.

He explored a single millimeter at a time, chasing the shadows that danced along my skin, while I tried to remember to breathe. Pulling me higher onto his lap, he pulled my back against his front until he absolutely surrounded me. For the life of me, I couldn't figure out why it had taken me this long to learn that his skin was softer than mine, or that he smelled like the sea pine right outside my grandparents' home.

My shivers intensified when he put his mouth to my ear and whispered, "You are so beautiful." He had said it so quietly, I asked him to say it again.

Emboldened by his whispers, I leaned my head back on his shoulder, barely trailing my lips along his neck until I found the pulse point right below his ear. There, I lingered just long enough to feel his heartbeat quicken.

And then, I kissed him again.

eight

FOR TWO WHOLE days after Darwen went down and the other boy's body was found, we were forced to stay out of the ocean. On the one hand, I felt grateful they were looking to link things together as more than separate random accidents, but on the other, the further disruption to my training schedule made me feel desperate.

Before summer had started, I had two training sessions each day. I alternated between swimming, surfing, paddling, and running. I'd planned to increase that to three sessions per day after First Night but, because of my injury, I'd barely managed one, and then only if Blake was with me.

Mica spent more and more time off Island and one of the days when our beach was closed, Blake and I tagged along with him to a surf spot he liked on the mainland. It was only twenty miles from Pinhold, but the change made for a completely different ocean. The water tasted saltier and looked more green than blue. The waves were huge and choppy, not like the smooth ones on Pinhold's shore.

After an hour in the water, I'd been knocked off my board so many times, I regretted coming out.

Then I got the wave. The kind you just know is coming even before it appears. I dropped in at the perfect point, I was steady on my board and I rode halfway into shore when a shadow came across my peripheral vision too close to me. I couldn't turn out of the way in time and a huge guy sliced across my board, knocking me into the foamy churn.

In spite of the powerful surf, I got back on the sand quickly. I was perfectly fine, but annoyed that the ankle strap to my board had been sliced.

"Cami, are you ok? I am so, so sorry. I didn't realize it was you," Jonas said running over with my board. We'd known Jonas forever. He was a nice guy, a couple years older than us and originally from Jamaica. He and his crew were known to be territorial about their waves, but not usually with Mica and me. He'd bailed on the wave to bring back my board, which made his apology genuine. "I'd 'a never cut you off on purpose if I'd 'a realized who you were," he mumbled, smiling as he shook the water out of his long dreads.

I smiled at Jonas, accepting his apology quickly because he was close with Mica, and I truly felt he hadn't meant to hurt me. But that wasn't good enough for Blake. I sensed his anger even before I heard his heavy steps on the beach running to me.

"You don't cut people on waves," Blake growled, running up suddenly. Without Jonas or me a chance to explain, he slammed his fist in Jonas' face, cutting off the rest of the apology. "You don't own the beach or the waves. Don't forget it again."

Too fast for me to stop it, another punch followed. The beads at the end of Jonas' hair clacked against each other and flew through the air with the contact. Jonas retaliated immediately with a fist of his own that caught Blake right on the eye.

"Stop!" I yelled, jumping in the middle of the two of them and pushing Blake back with every ounce of strength I had. "He was apologizing to me!"

That statement plus the hit got Blake to back off. He blinked a few times, wiping the blood from his eye, just as three big guys I didn't know ran our way. I worried Blake was about to get it. Jonas, bless him, stopped them in their tracks. Luckily, a big brawl was averted, but that quickly brought an end to our surfing.

On the ferry ride home Mica was furious at both of us. We made a tense triangle, alone on what should have been a crowded deck because, for the first time ever, Pinhold had red-flagged the beaches and sent incoming tourists back home. Mica stood on the bow of the boat staring into the chop that was jumping all the way up to the rails of the boat. Jagged walls of water bounced around him, in tune with the anger coming our way.

Blake sat on a bench a few feet over from me, leaning his head against the railing and using gravity to help hold an ice pack on his eye. The blood was gone, but condensation leaked down his face and his eye was already quite swollen.

I wanted to hug him. But, for the very first time, I felt torn between him and Mica. I paced back and forth between them, trying to figure out how to smooth over this very odd event.

"What on earth were you thinking?" I yelled at Blake.

"About Darwen and Shay, and how, if you went down, it would be all Jonas's fault," Blake said.

"But this was completely different, and I was up. And, he was apologizing!" I countered, confused. "It was an accident."

"No, he accidentally cut you, but he was perfectly willing to cut someone else off."

"Whatever, Blake," Mica cut in. "People cut all of us off, all the time, and you've never punched anyone because of it."

"Things are different now," Blake choked out, working hard to stop the anger from taking over his voice.

"I really hope you didn't do it for me," I said, "because I can take care of myself."

"Whatever, Cami," Mica snorted, eye roll obvious even behind the dark lenses of his Wayfarers. "You love it and you know it. Trying to pretend otherwise just makes it even worse."

I glared at him. It wasn't fair for him to share what was going on in my head about Blake in front of Blake. This was one of those times when I hated our twin link. He was right, and it was embarrassing.

Part of me felt bizarrely excited that Blake had decked a guy on my behalf. I should have felt upset at how quickly he turned to violence, or how he didn't let me fight my own battles, but I wasn't. Knowing he would stand up for me like that was hot.

I glared at Mica, and silently yelled at him to shut up.

"Stop talking in your heads!" Blake yelled. "I hate that."

"And I hate, that you guys are together, and everything has changed. We can't even have a single afternoon where we just hang out like normal and have a good time."

"Of course we can," I said. "We just did."

"No, we didn't. I have to see how you feel about him all the time. And you," he said right to Blake, "are equally obsessed. You jumped off a wave to get in a fight, over nothing. We never just hang out and have fun anymore. This summer sucks!"

It made me sad to know Mica felt left out, or jealous, or whatever, and hadn't said anything about it before today.

"Dude, I'm sorry if you've been feeling a little left out. But, as for a regular fun day, it's a little hard to go back to beach bum when Darwen and Shayla are in a coma and The Guard is continuing to look at the water to find out why two people have died," said Blake as he and Mica glared at one another.

"But, what happened to Shay and those guys didn't happen because something knocked them down," I said, hoping to shift the discussion from my relationship and onto the other, more important topics.

"How do you know?" Blake retorted. "We have no idea what happened. Shay definitely went underwater and didn't come up. I didn't want to watch that happen to you, too."

We got back on Pinhold to good and bad news. The beach would reopen the next day and they'd come to terms to continue the Surf Carnival, but the Pin had moved.

Billy explained that when they went to check the small Island today, the pin was tilting in a way that indicated things were not as balanced as they had been on First Night. With everything that had happened, it wasn't a huge shock, but since we still didn't know what caused the incidents in the water, Billy said The Guard was more freaked out than he'd ever seen them before.

"When they talked about stuff in the water, did anyone mention this?" Blake asked pulling a folded piece of faded paper from his pocket. The ink was blurry but still legible. "Fisherman's warning: intermittent testing in the area," I read, squinting, trying to see the dates.

"It was easier to read before it was in my shorts all day. I found this taped up on the ferry. But one of the dates was the day of the Ocean Swim," he said. "And there are more dates this week. I looked it up on my phone and it says there's been some research in Australia that ties sonar to some mass strandings there, so I thought maybe it could have something to do with what happened to Shay?"

"It's definitely worth looking into," Billy said, taking the paper and folding it back up again. "I need to go back to the hospital, but Celeste and I can meet up with you later today. I don't know much beyond the basics of sonar, but she might know something."

Blake and I combed through more information on his iPhone. "It seems to go both ways," Blake said, after reviewing a blog post from a Navy scientist who talked about dolphins seeking out test locations.

The blog talked about dolphins interrupting transmissions to come over and chat and play, ruining the data of many sessions. It also said that the dolphins got confused by these artificial noises that mimicked their bio-sonar. It went on about how dolphins could actually project physical force with their sonar, literally blasting the water around them to reveal abandoned warheads buried in the sand on the ocean floor. This physical force reminded me of the way the dolphin had aimed a blast of energy at me on First Night and stopped the bleeding on my head. It had seemed like an invisible wave that I really felt. Now, I understood this was the dolphin's sonar, projected at me.

"Do you think they were really trying to talk to the machines? The dolphins, I mean?"

"Hang on," Blake said. I watched his fingers click against the keyboard and thought about how good they'd felt on my skin the other night on my deck. I shook my head to clear the thought, because watching Blake go all serious and super-sleuth was sexy, too. "Regular sonar has been happening for years, and the dolphins seem to have adapted, but these research papers talk about some kind of more significant testing, so that would be something new, right?" he reported.

"But, what could that do to the dolphins?" Blake held up a finger while his eyes scanned the page. "It's possible that sonar can mess with the part of their inner ear that helps them regulate water pressure between dives. One theory is that it harms that tube and they go down instead of up, because they can no longer tell which direction is which."

"They breathe like we do, so wouldn't they need to surface eventually?" I wondered out loud.

"I don't know," Blake huffed, running his hand over his hair from back to front in frustration. "There are thousands of articles here, and I barely understand what I'm reading.

It could be a total waste of time, too. I mean, it would be pretty random for any of this to actually be related."

"Well, it's something. Celeste might know more. Let's just wait to talk to them," I said, getting up and brushing sand from my legs. I held up a hand to pull Blake from the floor, but instead he tugged me down on top of him. It might have taken me an extra minute to get up again, but I didn't mind. Not one little bit.

nine

IT WAS LATE by the time we met on the beach. French fries for dinner had become a frequent, if unhealthy, habit. But I couldn't stomach the hotdogs everyone else had grabbed. Any meat besides fish turned my stomach, lately. I plucked another French fry from the paper carton, wondering if the fuel of elite athletes could ever consist of protein shakes, fried potatoes, and gummie candy. I just hoped for a chance to find out.

Celeste ran the dolphin rescue truck to three different locations up and down the coast, all day. Hundreds of dolphins had beached, dying by the dozens, and no one had any idea why. I felt her weariness in my bones, but was grateful she hung out to talk. In spite of her exhaustion, Celeste had patience for our questions, perhaps because she felt frustrated, too.

"They certainly could swim up on the sand and get stuck if their directional instincts are messed up. It's definitely one current theory to explain the beachings. It's also possible most of them die in the ocean, and only half find their way out to shore. We just don't see the other half, so we don't have as much data," explained Celeste. She made a face, rolled her eyes up in her head a bit, like she was searching for answers somewhere up there. Not for the first time this summer, I was so glad I could come to her for help.

"I'm sorry," I said, passing her an open bag of candy. She took a few and smiled gratefully.

"Could sonar do that to humans?" Blake asked.

"It usually doesn't," Celeste continued. "But it does affect dolphins to some extent, even though I'm not sure it's to blame for any of the recent breachings or deaths."

"I remember reading that," Blake said, nodding. "Dolphins can use their echolocation to see through things; like an x-ray. Don't they call it bio-sonar?"

"Yes," Celeste said, shaking her curls from her eyes. In spite of the serious nature of our talk, it sparked something within her. I felt jealous that she had a career, something she'd pursued with a passion. My family had never encouraged that for me. I was meant to stay on the island, protect the ocean, and pass along our history. They never asked if I wanted something different than that. And that made me feel angry.

"So you agree sonar could be harmful to dolphins?" I asked.

"It does interfere with the way dolphins process information about the world," Celeste admitted.

"How?" Blake asked.

"We're still not sure exactly. One popular supposition is that the sonar crowds the signals they use to maneuver through the water and stay safe. With the extra noise, they can't accurately interpret their surroundings or warnings from their pod."

"What's the other one?" I asked. Celeste gave me a blank look. "You said one supposition. I assume that means there's at least one more?"

"Well, yes, some scientists believe that the sonar blasts can have a damaging effect on the dolphin's equivalent of an ear drum, mess up their depth perception, and can cause them to stay underwater for so long they essentially drown themselves."

"But, you don't think there's any way that's what's happening here?"

"Billy looked, extensively, for information on ear damage when you guys first brought this up, but he found nothing. It was a good idea, guys, really, but it doesn't translate to humans. We don't have bio-sonar; so the man-made sonar doesn't affect us in the same way."

"How can something be so damaging to the dolphins that's already part of their nature?" Blake asked.

"It's like the oil spill," I broke in.

Blake's curiosity turned me on, his questions exposing the intelligence he often kept in the background. He did well in school, but showing it off wasn't his thing. Kaleb had been the more intellectual one. But, like many siblings, especially twins, Blake chose other areas to excel in and different ways to get attention. His questions and ideas through this whole process had been incredibly insightful, especially today.

"You're right—the oil is natural: it's found in the ocean and on the beach," Celeste said, "but when there's a spill, like Deepwater Horizon, that's man messing with nature; it ruins the balance of things."

"To say nothing of all the crap they put in after the oil spill," Blake said. "Couldn't that be causing all this?"

"Anything's possible, guys, but nothing that's been found so far indicates that Shay or Darwen's conditions are being caused by that. I think more people would be susceptible if it were caused by chemicals, or from an oil spill. That, at least, is something that could affect humans. The sonar, really, isn't."

I'd been quiet for the most recent exchange; something was running around in my head, but to put words to it would make me seem even more nuts that I already did.

"About that—do the dolphins use sonar to talk?" I asked.

"Sort of. It's part of a bigger system; their clicks and whistles are more like talking, the way you and I do, but it's thought that they use their bio-sonar to communicate silently by sending images directly to each other's melons—you know, that big round spot on their heads."

"How do you know that?" Blake asked.

"We have extensive studies on sonar, on dolphins working together, and how it works," Celeste said.

"So, if people could do the same thing; wouldn't that be sonar?" I asked her.

"Like ESP? Or telepathy? Maybe," she said. "It does exist in nature, but still, sonar and people? I don't know of a link."

"What does all this have to do with Shay?" Mica asked, with a scowl.

"She passed out underwater," I said out loud. "Instant coma, remember? And, she was breathing. She didn't swim in the wrong direction and just not come up for air." I creased my brow in thought. "But, if sonar can hurt dolphins, maybe it can do the same thing to humans, even if it's not in exactly the same way." I was grasping at straws, but it felt important to continue pulling.

"They've been using sonar around here for years," Mica said, pacing. "Something would have happened before."

"But this was a significant enough test to warrant a warning to the fisherman. It's got to be something different," argued Blake. "What if it's like really loud music or something, which can hurt your ears; like that crazy broken squeal a speaker makes when it gets feedback? Last time that happened, I had a headache for days."

"There are different levels of sound waves," Celeste said in agreement, "and we have found some dolphins with burst ear drums. But, I agree with Mica. Even if this was causing the problems for the dolphins, which has never been proven exactly, it doesn't relate to humans."

"But we have strange ears," I exclaimed. Mica rolled his eyes. I'd obsessed over this detail when it was just Shay. Billy had investigated as he'd promised, and found some internal bleeding, but it obviously hadn't killed her like the dolphins. So, that knowledge hadn't helped explain the coma. Now that they had Darwen to compare it to, I hoped they might look into it again. It just felt significant to me, but I had no idea why.

"It would sound loud to us, Cami," Billy explained, kindly. "We don't use echolocation, or hear the same frequencies that dolphins do. I can look into sonar testing on humans to see if there is any proof that it affects the body. Maybe it can cause damage in some other way, but I've never come across that info before," he said, smiling gently. "If we find where it affects the brain, perhaps we can find a way to repair the damage. It's a long shot, but I'm willing to look into anything that seems like a realistic possibility. In any event, I arranged for a new MRI machine. It should be here in a few days."

Well, that made me feel a little better. The first one broke when they'd tried to examine Shay, but Alysha had said her parents didn't push through for a new one because, they thought Shay would wake up. I nodded, satisfied that there was forward motion of some kind.

Mica and Blake and I sat on the beach sharing French fries and soda—a gain—for dinner. We were making a habit of this far too much since Alysha had signed on to work at the snack bar. She was lonely with Shayla in the hospital and her parents around so much. Doc's son Helix was the manager at the snack bar, and he seemed to let her get away with murder. She took multiple dinner breaks and always brought tons of snacks.

It was hardly the chow of champions, but we were fighting to fit in as much training time as possible and needed the quickest fix of calories to refuel. I doubled up my training schedule, adding two surf sessions to the two hours of swimming I generally did, since I had missed so much time already.

Mica was an amazing surfer. He was almost better on the board than he was with swimming, and I think he loved it more. I actually preferred swimming. Surfing was fun, but I wouldn't have done it competitively if it wasn't an event in the Carnival.

"I totally don't get my parents at the moment," Alysha huffed. "It's like they've been replaced with robots, programmed to repeat Doc's nonsense over and over again."

"The way they act like he's God makes me sick," Mica said.

"Yeah, well you wouldn't even be here if it weren't for Doc," Blake said. "So, maybe he knows what he's talking about a little bit?"

"Maybe about making babies," Mica retorted, "but how could he know about this thing when it's never happened before?"

"They won't even say that it's a thing," she said. "'It's an accident. A coincidence. No further questions, please,'" she continued, doing an uncanny imitation of Doc's gravelly voice and Mainlander accent.

"My mom thinks they're in shock," I said.

"I think they're the ones who need a shock," she retorted, getting more upset by the minute. "They just sit around praying, begging the gods for Shay to wake up. I highly doubt that's what your mom would do if it were one of you in that bed."

"I definitely think she'd be more aggressive, considering we get blood drawn every time we get the flu," Mica agreed. "At the very least, she'd insist on blood tests and CAT scans up the wazoo. Speaking of, I didn't tell her about the blood Billy drew from us on the day of the race. Did you?"

"No. If she knew we didn't get the test results yet, she'd never let us in the water," I said, my voice dropping out, not needing to say more when Mica saw an old childhood memory flashing in my head and he showed me his version of the same event.

It must have been clear we were speaking silently, because Blake called us out on it. "Care to share with the class, kids?" The harsh angle of his raised eyebrow made it impossible to take his joke at face value.

He knew we were clicking to each other, and one look at Lysh's face told me she did too. Blake seemed annoyed, but it set Alysha crying and I felt awful for reminding her about what she was no longer able to do with Shay.

"Mom went psycho on this nurse until they called security," Mica said, filling everyone in.

"We were nine, and someone failed to call her with some routine test results," I explained. "She got out of control—and fast."

"Even though our mom almost got arrested, the nurse got canned when Doc came back," Mica added. "I was so embarrassed."

"Really?" I asked. I never knew this, and was shocked his emotional reaction that day was so different from my own. "I was pretty psyched to see her fighting—instead of worrying, for once."

"Well, maybe we should tell her about the blood test," Blake suggested. "Let's get her psycho in a way that helps out Shay and Darwen."

"Yeah, but we need to figure out what we can tell her that gets her to help, without worrying her so much that she puts Mica and me on lockdown," I said, grabbing Blake's forearm for just a second. My need to touch him—anywhere—grew like a thirst every time we were together.

I kept it brief, because more than two seconds would get me all distracted. Our constant tiny touches were completely necessary, yet totally unfulfilling. It was like a dehydrated person chomping ice when, really, only a gallon of water would do.

Blake's arm muscles twitched as I pulled away, chasing the spark we made together until the next moment when his knee found mine. This was as much as we could do right now.

Alysha and Mica noticed, but we all worked to stay focused on the topic at hand. Around us, the beach buzzed with day-trippers totally oblivious to the recent tragedies.

A lanky runner came over the sand at top speed. His legs moved in that circular run that is only possible on the forgiving surface of the beach. He fell twenty feet from us, face first into the sand. I jumped up to help, realizing as we got closer that it was Helix, Doc's son. He'd never seemed to like any of us very much, though it seemed he had softened to Alysha since she'd started working for him at the snack bar.

"I'm fine," Helix muttered into the sand, his pale face reddening the moment he realized he knew us. Helix was two years older than us and in college on the Mainland. It took a very long moment more until he caught his breath enough to sit and then stand. As soon as he could, he tried to get away from us, but he almost fell back on the sand. Blake caught him.

"Come sit on my board and we'll get you set," Blake said, helping Helix hop over to sit down while I dunked a towel in the ocean to wrap around his ankle.

"It's just twisted," Helix said, sitting with a sand-covered scowl. His hard mask softened minutely when he looked up to see Alysha. He gave her a nod.

"Man, people are getting busted up left and right around here," Mica said, tossing a surf sack. These were small cornstarch packets we used to get the sticky sand off of our skin. Helix caught the small square in a puff of white and started dusting the cornstarch over his face and arms. Like magic, the dark granules came off, but his sour look did not.

"Does that help?" I asked, avoiding Helix's unhappy face to wrap the wet towel around his ankle. If indeed it was only twisted, the salt water would quickly draw out the pain. Unfortunately, I didn't have a similar fix for his emotional discomfort. He was anti-social on a good day, which this so obviously was not.

"There's something very special in Pinhold saltwater," Blake joked, trying to make Helix more comfortable. I loved that he tried, even though Helix didn't seem to appreciate it.

"Oh my god! That's why they were blood testing you, right?" Alysha asked.

Mica and I looked at each other, unsure about continuing our discussion in front of Helix. He'd been quite the tattletale in our younger years. Whenever we were forced to play together, he'd tattle on us to our parents for every little thing and we spent the whole time in trouble. Mom claimed that as an only child, he couldn't be expected to know how to work things out for himself the way that we did and begged for our sympathy on his visits.

He was always the odd man out. Even though I felt bad about it, we'd stopped hanging out as soon as we became responsible for making our own plans. It was just no fun to get in trouble all the time.

Alysha clearly felt no such concern for his trustworthiness, continuing on as if we'd never been interrupted.

"I've been trying to figure out why I didn't get tested that day, too. I thought they were just being lax. But now I get it: I didn't get tested, because I didn't get wet."

Helix listened to Alysha, and his face showed some sympathy, which took the edge off things a little bit.

"So, they must have been thinking, at least initially, this wasn't a total coincidence," Blake mused. "Maybe we'll know more when the tests come back."

"Nothing unusual showed up," Helix said. "In your blood or in the water."

"So, why didn't they just tell us that?" Mica asked, conspiracy theories bouncing in his brain as he waxed his board, rubbing out his frustrations.

"My dad's not one for sharing 'unnecessary' information, in case you haven't noticed," Helix said, shrugging.

"Everything's necessary until Shay wakes up," Alysha said, looking at Helix like he had the answers to everything she needed to know in the world.

Helix blushed. "I can help you out. I can't exactly give the test results to you, but I can file transfer them to Billy. What time does he get home tonight?" Helix asked.

Blake answered and we made a plan to meet up online later. To make the transfer work, Billy had to be at home and ready to download some files from Doc's computer so we made a plan to reconvene at Billy and Blake's house after dark.

"Maybe he didn't call you because, he just didn't find anything," Billy hypothesized, ready to minimize the open window on his home computer after Helix had texted us that it was ready.

Helix made the test results available to Billy by simply switching the access settings on Doc's home computer. It seemed strange, him helping us like this, but Billy learned from working in Doc's office that father and son were at odds, at the moment. And, in any event, looking at the files this way wouldn't leave any kind of trail, because Billy was often in the general system.

Billy and Blake's basement was always a favorite study spot, for school or any of the tests we needed coming up through the Junior Guard. It provided comfort, even now as we struggled to make connections between what Helix was giving us and what Billy was seeing at the hospital. The cool blue tones that decorated the walls and furniture did nothing to calm my racing heart. For once, at least lately, the extra beats per minute were not because of Blake. Even though only our own test results were up on the screen, and even though Billy technically had a right to examine the files as a resident, what we were doing felt a little shady.

"Maybe he didn't want anyone to know he did all these tests, because the results didn't come back with anything relevant," said Celeste, following on Billy's theory. We brought her up to speed on everything when she joined us after work. Alysha went to the hospital, so it was just the five of us there.

"Do ours match Shay's?" Mica asked, like a dog with a bone. He wouldn't—couldn't—let go of the idea that something more was going on here.

"I'll look, but only if you go sit on the couch. I can't have you over my shoulder on this one," Billy said, pointing to the comfy white cushions that completed the nautical theme and had stayed miraculously pristine over ten years in a house with boys.

He opened all the test results and started comparing ours to Shay's, jotting a couple notes on a legal pad, while I tried to keep from fidgeting.

Calm Down. We're just checking our own files, Mica said quietly in my head, sending me calming imagery that did absolutely nothing to assuage my guilt.

What about Shay's? And Darwen's? I clicked back.

Doc knows something about this that he's not saying. We have to find out somehow, he answered back, directly into my brain.

He was right. I didn't know why I felt that way, without any real proof. If I stopped arguing, maybe Billy could come up with something to make it true. Still, my worried instincts weren't enough to justify snooping in medical records. That went beyond wrong and somewhere into illegal.

While Mica's thoughts got me even more agitated, Blake's actions had me distracted. The small circles he made on my lower back quieted my external jitters, but further accelerated my racing pulse.

With an eye roll and a smile, Mica popped off the couch and grabbed a beanbag starfish from a 'moment' Blake's mom had set up. It was one of many around their house; objects combined with color and picture to draw your eyes around the room. Knowing she had three boys, Blake's mom had gone out of her way to put touchable items in with the fragile ones. She figured if she gave her boys an obvious grab, they'd leave the delicates alone. So far, it had worked.

Mica beaned the bag to Blake who caught it one handed and sent it back. They exchanged it almost ten times before Billy stopped writing. Celeste was looking over Billy's shoulder at the pad.

"Nothing, right?" he said to her.

"Nothing new, chemically. Some elevated nitrous and a lot of extra particles of ceridium—all of that is consistent with their tests from the past year or so. But why on earth have Cami and Mica had so many tests?" she asked, grabbing the notes from Billy's hand.

"Don't you know we're precious?" Mica sneered.

"That's what our mom used to say when we cried about the needle pricks," I explained.

"Okay, yes, we can all agree you're special, but there are almost one hundred records of tests from just the two of you," Celeste responded. "The same seems to be true for the other sets of twins, too."

"You know about the years of infertility?" Billy asked.

Celeste nodded.

"Your mom told me," she said to him. "And we have some research on it at the center."

"Why would you have information on that in a lab about the ocean?" Blake asked.

"It coincided with a time of very low dolphin births."

We knew the numbers of dolphins in the water had diminished, which was one of the reasons The Guard voted to lease land to the center. But, I had never considered parallels in the timeline before.

"Do they know why?" I asked.

"BPA in the water," she said. "That's the theory, anyway. It was never proven one way or the other because the research money got spent on fertility studies instead."

"That was right around the beginning of Plastic Isle," Billy said, nodding. "I never thought about that before."

"At the time, no one knew that BPA could interrupt gene development and fertility. All that research came later. But, we do know that in the eighties, the Plastic Isle grew big enough that it started to influence ocean currents, sending streams of water towards the Island.

"But if the pollution reached us, wouldn't it have reached the Mainland, too?" Blake asked.

"It has, it's just happened much more slowly," said Celeste. "It may be that you're in a more direct stream of pollution, because the currents around the Island that bring the big waves also bring other things. Additionally, you practically live in the water and eat fish almost exclusively for protein. Just like dolphins."

"Just us and the dolphins?" joked Mica. "Maybe we do share DNA."

"Well, we all share DNA," Celeste said, taking Mica's joke seriously. "I mean, scientifically speaking. They're at the top of the food chain, have brains even bigger than ours, and they process toxins in a similar way," she said.

"Yes," Billy continued, "and I can tell you from time on the Mainland that the same conditions are being seen by the medical community there. But, it definitely seems to happen faster and more dramatically to the population here."

"So, it's almost like we're a stepping stone between the dolphins and the rest of the world?" Blake asked, making sense of it before I had made that connection.

"But what does that have to do with all the tests?" I asked, eager to focus back on the medical records while we still had access to them. We didn't know how long Helix would feel like helping.

Billy shrugged, but Celeste brushed a rusty curl behind her ear and looked thoughtful. "It's possible that they know this, and are making sure you're all in the clear for some of the pollutants and conditions we're seeing in the dolphin population."

"Isn't that a little creepy? Doing tests on people because of what's happening with animals?" Mica asked.

I shook my head, disagreeing with my twin. "Whatever happens to the dolphins will happen to us." It was one of the tenants we learned about the ocean and the signs regarding the balance of the Pinhold pin.

"That's just Junior Guard mumbo jumbo," Mica argued.

"I'm afraid not. Just with those dolphin deaths yesterday, we lost a couple of degrees on the Pin," Billy said.

I gasped because, although I knew it had tilted, I didn't actually think it was tied to the dolphins.

"Look, you guys need to understand. The things you can't see are often just as real as the things you can," Billy explained.

Celeste shrugged. "I can't know why they've done all these tests for so many years, but I can tell you for a fact that dolphins are a sentinel species. We watch them very carefully, because, eventually, what happens to them will happen to us."

After scouring the medical records, Mica, Billy, and Celeste left Blake and me for some much-appreciated alone time. It was funny how much I craved that, when before, I'd avoided being alone with him because of that strange undercurrent that had fluttered between us…which I always thought was Kaleb.

For a blissful hour, we snuggled on the couch and watched reruns while I attempted to forget everything but that moment. Laid out against him on the nubby white fabric, I could finally give in to my need to touch him for longer than five seconds at a time.

Every time I tried to talk about something other than the angst on screen, Blake silenced me with a kiss. The couch was barely big enough for us both, but his strong grip kept me squashed against him in all the very best places.

The hard muscle in his arms surrounded me as I snuggled into his side and relished the constant contact I'd craved.

One of my newly-discovered favorite spots to explore was the bare skin on his head that matched my own. In the past few days, a tiny bit of stubble had grown in on our matching wings, so light I could barely see it. I couldn't stop running my fingers over it, going against the way the hair grew so the little bits of rough pushed against my fingers.

I kept my cheek right under the crook of his neck and took him in with all five senses. Long golden blond eyelashes framed amazingly mismatched eyes. Sunscreen and cornstarch, the smells of our childhood, mixed with the spicier scents of sea grass and salt water that had me drooling until I got brave enough to take a taste. I pressed a kiss to the skin under his ear, which caused him to squirm against me in the most delicious way. It was clearly a hot spot for him, and I couldn't resist doing it again, and again.

We moved to get closer together every way that we could; his legs and hips and chest moved against me until we built a rhythm. It made me think about the way his body moved in the water the other day, which made me heat up from the inside, out. A deep blush rose on my skin, and I felt grateful that he couldn't read my mind. Although, with the way my body responded, he really didn't need to. He cupped my face with strong, square hands and brought our lips together.

Everything burst in waves of color and sound simultaneously. It pulsed like lightning behind my eyes, reverberating over and over again, so brightly it felt like I could see the same image inside Blake's head, too.

ten

THE SATURDAY OF the Relay Competitions came around faster than I expected. It began with hazy, gray skies, but the sun finally made an appearance. Now, it shone almost too bright for me—the clouds had suited my mood because I wasn't ready for this event. The Guard and the Surf Lifeguarding Commission were arguing over new regulations for the Surf Carnival events, given the two deaths in the Ocean Swim. They moved the relay up, because it didn't require any long distance swimming and people worked on teams, so they felt the danger was mitigated a bit. For many, these events were the most fun in the Surf Carnival. They moved fast, had many winners, and awarded multiple certifications, depending on how may competitions we did.

I'd originally planned to take part in only two. The Dash & Swim should have been an easy competition for me, one I'd won frequented as a Junior. But this time, I came in third.

"The difference between first and third was four seconds," Blake said to me after I'd finished my heat. "And you missed over a week of training, so don't be too hard on yourself." Pep talks from Blake at competitions weren't new to me. He'd been captain of the Junior Guard team, and the role of cheerleader came naturally to him. But this was the first competition where I wanted him around on a different level. While I wasn't about to start a full-on PDA at the event, I couldn't stop the tiny touches that meant almost as much as the PDAs, to me.

The Canoe Relay was always fun because, we got to compete as a team of seven, going backwards in the waves. While it required an iron stomach and quick hands, it was one event that we trained for extensively together. We were down Shay and Darwen, who we had practiced with, so Billy and Stella were in the canoe with us. I hated Stella because of the way she'd flirted with Blake at the pool right after we got together. As the most experienced of the group, they sat in the two seats facing us.

It was bad form to turn around and look at the waves, so we took cues from their expressions. When their eyes got big, we knew there was a big wave coming from behind. Using all my senses, I felt and heard where it came from in order to steer my portion of the boat in the most advantageous way. There were twelve boats in the water, besides ours. Three capsized in the big waves, and we ended up coming in second. It wasn't too bad, considering we'd only practiced with Stella once.

The Rescue Relay competition wasn't my strong suit. It required knee boarding, lassoing an object with a buoy, and dragging it back in. It was the middle part that caused me so much trouble. And I had all day to worry about it. Last-minute instructions from Mica crowded my brain. For extreme rescuing, we needed to know how to lasso like a cowboy, and my brother was an expert. His dude ranch was the entire ocean. He caught fish by tossing nets, while I struggled to wrap the silly rope around a pole.

I stood off to the side, waiting for my heat to begin. A combination of nerves and the newly bright sun brought tears to my eyes. I held them in, seeing prisms on the sea as the sun picked that moment to dip into the afternoon sky. A thousand points of light dispersed, bounced off the water and burned. I kicked the sand, angry with myself for forgetting the shaded goggles I usually wore on days like this.

It hadn't mattered in the earlier events, but now, when I had my hardest challenge, the bright light made me more nervous. When Blake bopped up to me, I no longer had to pretend my tears were caused by the sun, because they were. I couldn't see a thing over the water, and I felt my chance for lassoing the buoy and reeling it in, was nil. It was going to make me lose the whole thing.

Blake moved to the beat in his head that always seemed loudest before a meet. It was one of the things that used to drive Kaleb crazy, because he had to hear it too, every time Blake got ready for a competition. They both had drummer's disease: always using whatever surface around as a drum. He took off his shaded goggles after I explained the reason for my tears.

"They're my lucky pair," he said, placing them over my eyes. He secured the seal and then carefully drew the band down over my hair—trying not to grab any loose strands in the process—and pulled my ponytail through.

His hands were quick and firm as he adjusted the fit and I forgot all about why they were there on my temples and focused only on the gorgeous guy in front of me who suddenly looked silver. The borrowed goggles were exactly the color my dolphin's eyes had been. I wondered if this was how we looked to her. I thanked him with a quick kiss on the cheek that stuck to my single-second-of-touching rule.

"That's all I get for my lucky goggles?" he asked.

"For now," I said with a wink that didn't quite work and that he didn't see, considering my eye was surrounded by plastic.

"Okay," he smirked. "I wouldn't want to distract you."

"Jerk!" I punched him, but I was laughing, which was light years away from my freak-out just minutes earlier.

With the light shaded from my eyes, I focused on the competition. I recognized most of the other swimmers in my heat. The Guard had two members competing in the female race. Both were much older, closer to my mom's age, and in it to have fun. I felt confident I had the knee boarding part locked. Hopefully that could buy me extra time if I couldn't lasso the buoy the first or second time.

Just take it slow, Mica sent, reminding me of the frustration I felt before. His well-intentioned thoughts had the opposite effect. I had calmed myself down—with Blake's help—but now I felt myself begin to freak out again. Unfortunately, there weren't too many places I could run from a person who could come into my brain. Instead, I focused on absorbing as much of his knowledge as I could. His confidence calmed me in a way his advice couldn't.

With my brother in my brain, and my boyfriend's goggles on my face, I was ready when the gun went off. I took off on my knees, paddling as quickly as possible in the water, getting out in front of most of the pack right away. I ignored the sun, the crowds, and the other competitors to spot the target one hundred yards away. The ring strapped on the front of my board became my focus as I approached the target. I got close enough and tossed the ring, missing by a couple feet. I pulled it back to me and tossed it again. This time, a wave interrupted and I missed by just inches.

Pulling the ring back, I looked around. There were others approaching their buoys, and one person was already headed back. I took a deep breath and closed my eyes this time, remembering what my previous throws had felt like. This time, when I threw, I knew instinctively that I had it even before the ring hit. I pulled back with enough force to capture the buoy but not lose it again, secured the lasso to the ring, and turned my board back to the shore. With every ounce of strength in my arms, I pulled the board, the buoy, and myself to shore, and came in third. Not first place, as I would have liked, but much better than I'd feared.

At day's end, they handed out the certs for each event and tallied up all the various scores for ranking in the Surf Carnival as a whole, so far. I placed seventh for the day, twentieth overall. Which was ok, considering I had a big fat zero for the first event. Mica took third place for the day, and second overall, so far. Mica had killed it with the buoy, snagging it from thirty feet out, saving a ton of time and placing first in that event. Blake had missed his buoy completely, coming in twelfth for that event, which brought him down to fifth overall for the day, and fifth for all of the events in the Surf Carnival, so far.

Blake gave Mica a fist bump and silently walked down the beach with just a tiny wave to me. I started off after him, but Mica stopped me with a thought and a grab to my elbow.

Don't follow him. He needs to get his mad out, Mica insisted. "Let Blake walk off the loss," Mica said out loud.

You have no idea what he needs from me, I insisted to him, shaking my head in silence.

Maybe not. But I do know what he needs after a race— let him be by himself. Twelfth is tough to take when you're used to winning. Mica emphasized his silent communication with a warning look.

But one of you is always losing to each other, so why is he so pissed right now?

"Blake and I don't lose to each other. We're partners. Our competition makes us each work harder, get better," he said out loud.

"Like me and Shay," I said softly, fully understanding what he was saying.

Three weeks into this thing with Blake and me, and this was the first time Mica had attempted any interference. He'd been remarkably tight lipped, to the point that it seemed like he was almost censoring his thoughts on the relationship. He knew both of us better than he knew almost anything else in the world.

Mica reminded me of quite a few times when Blake lost and was forced too quickly to interact with people. It inevitably ended with a fight of some kind. Blake wasn't a loose cannon, running around beating people up, but he was too emotional and amped after a loss to do anything but lash out physically. A year, or so, ago, he'd had a rough racing season, and he had gotten in enough fist fights with opposing team members he was actually suspended. It had been the first time he'd gotten in trouble since Kaleb left.

I hadn't considered that there was a trigger there, but Mica clearly knew. Looking back though memories, I realized how often Mica had sequestered Blake after a loss. Since they were few and far between, I'd never made the connection. I'd always thought it was a post-race strategy session, and annoyingly obsessive on Mica's part. But now, I understood. I gathered up my things and headed over to my grandfather and his friends, letting Mica take care of my boyfriend.

A FEW NIGHTS later, Blake and I decided to get some information from a different authority. We found Gramps in The Guard's outpost by the Pavilion, drinking scotch with Stoney and two of their buddies. We asked to speak to our grandfathers alone—not wanting the others to hear, especially if my idea was just plain nutty. Instead of clearing my head, the walk over had me backtracking with my new theory. It was only Blake's support, and the comfort of his hand on my back, that kept us moving in the right direction.

Gramps took one look at my face, all shaky and pale from being in the hospital, and asked that the others leave us for a few moments. Stoney nodded, agreeing silently with the request. Like Blake, he didn't need to talk to demonstrate authority. Like the old-fashioned gentlemen they were, the other men deferred to my wishes with no questions asked.

"Gramps, the secret swirl the other day, does it mean anything else?" I asked hesitantly.

"It means everything, child. I told you; look and you'll find it everywhere," he said.

I nodded as he was speaking, "I found it, alright." I took a breath to steady myself, trying to find the words, "Did you know..." I stuttered, "I mean..." I stumbled, not sure what to ask. Blake looked at me and nodded, lending his strength silently. I began again. "Did you know that me and all the other twins born our year . . . did you know that we all have the same ears?"

Gramps' eyes opened in examination, but not surprise. He glanced casually at the side of my head, then at Blake's, and then at Stoney and nodded. With a gentle hand under my chin, he directed my eyes to his head as well. His were like mine.

"You have them, too?" I whispered in awe, looking over at Blake, whose face showed similar shock.

"Why the surprise, child? You know we're related, you and me."

"I thought... I mean, we thought that it meant something—something that could help Shay. Like something was wrong with our ears? Or something." Saying it out loud made me feel stupid.

I had felt so sure we were on to something important. But in over two weeks, Billy hadn't been able to connect it to anything that could help.

"It does mean something. You and I aren't the only ones related," Gramps said.

"Many of the old bloodlines have been combined and shared. That's what happens when people live in the same location for so many generations," Stoney explained.

I nodded, understanding, as did Blake, who got a slightly sick look on his face.

"Don't worry, young one," Stoney said to Blake with a wink. "There's not blood between you close enough to stop you two from being together." Um, Ew. And, phew. "There are many physical traits we share on-Island. Our ears are only one similarity. It's one of the things that makes us such good swimmers," Gramps added.

"How is that, sir?" Blake asked.

"Well, I don't know exactly, but it seems Mainlanders don't have such an easy time of going between air and water; they get earaches. Rufus out there can explain it better than I can. If you'd care to let him and Eli come back in here, we can ask them."

As the red in my face diminished, I nodded. It seemed nothing we had to discuss was that groundbreaking. I guess we didn't need privacy. I'd known Rufus and Eli my whole life, after all. Despite the initial disappointment, I still felt that new information was good information.

My grandfather gave a familiar whistle. Eli and Rufus whistled back about thirty seconds before they walked back in. They sat as if they had never left. Considering how fast they got back, I wondered if they had ever been far enough away to matter, anyway.

"Rufus, these children here just noticed that our ears are a bit unusual. Got anything to say about that?" Stoney asked.

Rufus looked at Eli and back at Gramps, almost as if he was seeking the other elder's permission before he started to talk.

"They help us care for the ocean, along with our skin and eyes. They make it possible to live in between the land and sea," Rufus said. "Weren't you paying attention in Nippers?"

I thought back, remembering Kaleb's snarky commentary more than the actual lesson.

"They'll tell us anything to keep us here, but these old stories don't mean anything," Kaleb had said. I pictured him so clearly in my head. I compared my memory of Kaleb and Blake at that age, with Blake standing in front of me now. Back then; they wore mostly the same kind of clothes, though Kaleb veered towards darker colors, with rips everywhere. Blake always looked like he'd walked off of a poster for sailing. He still did, but I really liked that now. Blake's ears hadn't seemed to change in size at all.

"Sorry," I answered. "I didn't get it then—we were small and they were just legends. I didn't think there was any truth in there." I trailed off. How could I explain how much of those lessons I'd ignored?

"If you're only focused on what you can see, you'll never learn anything," Stoney said.

I nodded. That lesson became more obvious every day. Nothing we'd seen so far had done anything to help the current situation.

I looked at my hand, wrapped in Blake's. There was nothing similar there. My skin was intensely tan like that of many, but not all, our people. Blake's was a softer gold and covered with the freckles of his very Irish-looking Dad. Both our families had been on-Island for many years. Still, we did have a variety of different ethnicities somewhere in our DNA, like many families did.

"It's not the color," Stoney continued, his voice so low, I felt the need to lean forward to hear him. "But the texture. Notice how smooth—like the skin of a pearl—how hairless it is? With nearly invisible pores?"

While noticing Blake's skin had certainly become a recent favorite pastime of mine, these were details I considered important and awesome on him. I never thought to compare them to myself. Hearing Stoney talk, I realized that the similarity was certainly there.

"And our eyes, although it's not true about mine," Rufus interjected, blinking his own brown ones for what felt like the first time since he'd come back in the room. "Those with the silvery-gray eyes, like yours Cami, or yours, Blake, have the ability to see easily and clearly underwater. They resist the sting of saltwater that forces many others, myself included, to use goggles or close our eyes."

"But, I wear goggles all the time," I said, immediately wondering why I said that.

"Because you need them, or because you just do?" asked Gramps.

Blake and I looked at each other, both considering what Gramps asked.

"I need them in the pool," I started.

"But not in the ocean," Blake finished. "When you found Shay you didn't have them on, did you?

I nodded and blinked a few times, trying to remember. "The water must have been very clear that day," I said slowly, trying to recall everything from that day. I remembered the buzzing when I first sensed Shay had a problem, before I'd known it for sure. That kind of vague prediction was zinging through me right now.

"Either the water has been much clearer these past few days, or you're seeing underwater better all the time."

"Is that possible?" I wondered aloud.

Blake nodded. "Yes, it's actually my normal. I never considered it anything special. Come to think of it, it does seem to be improving."

"If you get in The Guard, we help you develop it even more," Stoney said with a pointed look at Gramps. "It helps for rescuing."

I shuffled my feet uncomfortably. These were things we weren't supposed to know yet. But given the circumstances, it seemed like we needed to if the information could help Darwen and Shay. Stoney's eyes were deep silver like my own, even though his ears weren't the sacred swirl.

"These common traits are just like anything else you see in a family, among cousins and generations. They appear in some people, and not others, and they're more developed in some people than others," Stoney said.

"I could always see underwater," Gramps said, "but when I started diving, I got better."

"Me, too," Eli agreed. "And, not just that. The Mainlanders had to regulate, remember? But, we never did."

"Of course. It got to where I could go deeper, for longer, than any of the other guys we dove with," Gramps bragged.

"It's true," admitted Eli. "No matter how much I practiced, I could never beat your grandfather. And, no matter how much they practiced, the Mainlanders couldn't come close to us; not with holding their breath, sheer speed, or simply diving down deep."

Gramps nodded. "We're built to not get the bends. It seems to be hereditary."

Blake and I looked at each other.

"And dolphins are the same, right?" I asked, directing the question to Gramps.

"Well, legends say we do share this gift with our brothers and sisters of the ocean," Gramps answered.

"What about the science of all this?" I pressed.

Gramps raised an eyebrow at me. "I study dolphins in the water, not in a lab. Why do you ask?"

I took a deep breath, feeling a slight link between what I had come here thinking and what I had heard.

"We read dolphins can be affected by sonar. It can mess up the part of their ears that helps them calculate depth," I said, tripping over my words in an effort to link them together in a way that made sense. I felt a squeeze on my hand, and I took a breath, grateful Blake was there.

"We were wondering if maybe the same thing happened to Shay?" Blake questioned.

"And, if we all have the same ears as her," I continued, "we're worried the same thing could happen to all of us."

"Well, sonar's been used all over for lots of years, so it's really unlikely that's what hurt your Shay," Stoney said, "but I think you're sweet trying to help her out."

He patted Blake on the back in that strange half-hug guys exchanged. It felt like they were dismissing us like little kids who wanted to build a boat out of popsicle sticks.

I looked at my grandfather; sure he would understand that it wasn't just the sonar I was getting at here. But instead, he stood, kissed my cheek, shook Blake's hand, and shuffled us out the door without even a 'thanks for stopping by'.

Blake and I walked hand-in-hand along the water's edge. It was the pebbly part of the beach, and we were barefoot, but it didn't bother us.

"Guess they forgot to mention the super feet, huh?" Blake said, seeming for just the moment to read my thoughts.

"Remember the boat Kaleb wanted to build out of the connecting blocks?" I asked. "I didn't believe it would work."

"Yeah, I didn't either," Blake said. "But Kaleb knew, and he was right."

"We're onto something, too. I feel it. I'm just not sure what exactly the connection is."

"Kaleb would help if he was here. This is the kind of thing he's really good at. I'm sorry I'm not, but I'll help you in any way I can. I think you're amazing."

And then he kissed me. Not just a regular smooch, as if any of the ones with him ever were, but a bone-melting, wave-crashing, birds-singing type of kiss that left me breathless and desperate to do it again.

Seconds, minutes, hours later, my lips stung and my heart pounded.

Perhaps we were no closer to figuring out what was going on with our friends, but I felt better. My thoughts, which had been scrambled before, suddenly crystallized.

"If all these genes skip around—like with Rufus and Stoney and Gramps and Eli—how come in our generation it's all the same?"

Before Blake could answer, a call came from the ocean. Happy sounds, an invitation.

The beach had been open for two days, and I really wanted to go in. I couldn't resist the chance to swim with them again, this time with Blake. I couldn't resist the chatter. Grabbing Blake's hand, I dragged him into the sea.

Diving through waves lit only by moonlight, we rushed through the water to beyond the swells where I saw the dolphins hanging out. When we came up for air, on the other side of the wave break, we paused to get our bearings. Then, we treaded water with our heads above the sea. A sudden bump on my hip made me jump a bit.

I laughed and shot water at Blake, sure he had been the one to knock me. And then I saw his hands above the water. He splashed me back when I felt the bump again.

Looking down, I saw moonlight glinting off of unusually white dolphin skin. She'd come to find me, along with the dolphin Blake had played with that night by the dock at my house. They raised their heads above water, chattering happily then dipping below the surface. After three repeat performances we followed them.

It only took a few tries to get used to doing the free dives that took us ten feet, or so, below the surface where the dolphins played. Each time I went down, it seemed like I could hold my breath longer. My eyes adjusted to the depth of the water and the dark. The dolphins made bubbles big enough for us to swim through. They nudged us together to get us to kiss, and kept coming to the surface with us every time we needed air. Soon more of the pod joined us, and headed out to sea. We got nudged along until we got the hint and began to swim with them.

Underwater, the differences between various dolphins looked more obvious to me: their slight distinctions in color and shape, their swimming styles, personalities. A particularly agile and fast dolphin of very light blue loved to race. She kept my girl and me on the move in a friendly competition until we had gone miles out to sea. In the beginning, I had held on to her fins to cover the long distances. Then I caught her slipstream, like I had on First Night, remembering to come up more frequently for air than she did.

I'd felt safe in the water, which may have been a bit reckless, considering Darwen and Shay. But when we got so far that I couldn't see the lights on land, I began to worry. As if she knew how I was feeling, she made some noises, slipped underwater, and started swimming back toward land. Blake and the dolphin he'd been swimming with did the same thing.

Fifty feet from land, she stopped suddenly, and I came up to breathe. Blake did the same thing. We weren't actually close to Pinhold proper, but by the old lighthouse. Built on a rocky ledge, it had been part of the Island until an earthquake had pulled it away.

"I've never been over here," I said, almost reverently, surprised breathing came easy even after such a fast swim.

"Me, either," Blake said, shaking his head. "And, I have tried," he admitted. Adamantly off limits, the riptides surrounding it were the worst around Pinhold. Until this summer, the last two drowning deaths had happened right here.

My dolphin nudged me deeper into the water and led me closer to the structure, stopping in front of what looked like a door. Blake caught my eye and motioned that he saw it too. He pointed to a small porthole window and we swam over. We surfaced, took huge breaths and dunked under water. The space inside was filled with small, blinking lights. Nothing moved, which came as a bit of a relief. Blake swam back toward the door and gave a tug on the handle.

Magnified under water, the creaky squeak of unused door joints made a huge noise the dolphins didn't like.

Much to their obvious consternation, Blake tried again. Though the knob turned, the door didn't budge. It did, however, sound an alarm that was so loud it made the creak of the door sound like a whisper. Immediately, water flooded with light.

The sound burned my eardrums; so loud I saw it in my brain. My dolphin shook her head, as if trying to shut the noise out. Even with the visible discomfort, she didn't swim away. She pushed in between Blake and me and rubbed her fins against us until we got the hint. When we each grabbed one, she took off at a terrifying speed.

In a furious flash of fins and waves, Blake and I landed by my dock, out of breath, standing in water waist deep. My entire body shook with fear and exhaustion. Blake and the dolphin both appeared affected as well. It felt like we'd escaped from a crime scene. My dolphin had saved me again. Overwhelmed with gratitude, I wished for the ability to communicate how I felt with words, either hers or mine, but none came. It would have been easier if she was like Mica, and able to glimpse thoughts and feelings from pictures inside my brain.

I felt our connection had increased a thousand fold as I watched her swim away. Similarly, my feelings for Blake had expanded exponentially.

"If I had gone through that alone, I'd be doubting my sanity right now," I said, looking over at him.

"I'm still a little scared. It looked like some sort of lab to me," Blake said.

I nodded in agreement. "It could be a headquarters of some sort, but there wasn't enough room for a lot of people," I said, giggling a little bit. I knew we needed to sort out what we had seen, but at the moment my brain couldn't handle it.

On emotional and physical overload, I needed something to ground me. I moved towards Blake, desperate to touch him. Right now, only he made sense to me. It seemed he felt the same way. Endorphins raced through both of us, pulsing my way, drawing me with that same magnetic current that had linked us since First Night.

With every heave of his chest, each hitch of breath, my thoughts moved from everything we had seen to only what was right in front of me. Soaking wet, his black tee clung to every muscle. My own tank and shorts had made it easy to swim, but now clung like dolphin skin. Every nerve in my body felt exposed under the tight fabric and Blake's gaze.

Fear and flight turned into something equally intense that had my heart beating even faster. I needed to share these feelings with him, and I knew exactly how to do it. Suddenly, a one foot distance was too much. In the exact same instant, we flew at each other. Power and energy met in the middle, forcing the water that had been between us into a big wave that crashed around us as my lips met his.

Mouths, hands, fingers went everywhere. His and mine. I no longer recognized the separation between us, couldn't remember why we needed space, or clothes or air.

I stripped us off all these things, dragging him underwater over and over again to kiss him beneath the waves, in the one spot in the world that had always been mine and mine alone before. I didn't want to come up, not even to breathe. I became less conscious of the need, only aware of him.

But we didn't drown in any way. Instead, we separated, surfaced quickly and came back down again. It added just a little something, this synchronicity, like once again our cellular systems had connected beyond anything that made sense consciously. We were together, even on the most basic level.

I let go of everything except the water, and him, and truly, finally, let his love come all the way in. He took everything that I gave gratefully, and gave back even more. More love, more need, more feels. This thing between us moved beyond making me feel more alive. It had taken on a life of it's own.

THE NEXT DAY passed in a flurry of training sessions and beach patrol. At sunset I caught up to Mica and gave him the down low.

"Sounds like you found the Doc's secret lair," Mica said in a voice like a mustached villain from some old movie, making me laugh. "I knew he had one. Now, we just need to find out what he's hiding."

"There's something hidden there; otherwise, we'd have known, at the very least, that the place existed."

"I can ask Gram about it," I insisted, sure that the person I'd counted on for truth my entire life couldn't possibly be hiding a secret that was hurting our friends.

"You already told me Gramps and company sent you away as soon as you stopped the commentary and started with the questions. Why would Gram be different? They all know something. We have to get in there to see what they are hiding."

The smooth swoosh of the patio doors announced our mom's arrival. Like a movie soundtrack, we had warning to stop talking. I was grateful Mica was too interested in what I had to tell him to pick a fight that would keep her out there any longer than necessary.

"I'm glad you guys are home. We're having Gram, Doc, and Helix over for dinner tonight. Doc's worried Helix has been especially alone this summer. I expect you to be friendly," she insisted, staring at Mica.

Have fun! I have dinner plans with Blake, I told him silently.

Like a date? He questioned. *Not any more, you don't.*

"Helix is fine, Mom," Mica said, managing to keep the belligerence off his face.

"Really?" she asked, looking my way for confirmation.

"We hung out with him last week," I said, wondering what she'd think if we told her we'd been getting illegal access to Doc's files.

"Besides, we're grabbing dinner with Blake, so we're going out in twenty," Mica added, with a pointed look in my direction.

Jerk, I sent, shouting in silence, careful to keep the matching reaction from my face.

His sneaky two-pronged attack, meant to foil my plans and get himself out of dinner alone, only worked a little.

"So, have Blake come over here," said my Mom in a tone that broached no argument. "But, I expect you to include Helix in your activities. If you want to go out afterwards, then Helix will go, too."

Mica and I both cringed. My plans for Blake definitely did not include Helix or Mica. And Mica got a glimpse of what I had planned for Blake.

"Maybe they should be a little less worried about Helix and a little more worried about Shay," said Mica, out loud, unfortunately.

"Mica!" Mom said. "Doc is under enough pressure here with things you couldn't possibly understand. I expect you to treat him respectfully, because of who he is and also, simply, because he's a visitor in our home. Nothing else will be tolerated. Is this clear?"

"Yes, ma'am," Mica said in a conciliatory voice that hid the sneak attack he'd already plotted in his head.

"This is delicious, Lydia," Doc said when we were all seated at the dining table, inhaling food from a fork stuffed with a disgusting combination of salmon, peas and potatoes. For such a skinny guy, he'd put away an amazing amount of food in the sixty seconds since we'd said grace.

"Guess you don't have much time for good meals with all those extra hours at the hospital lately," I said, trying to find a way to make the most of the forced socialization.

"Or at the lab," Mica said.

So much for delicately drawing him out. Slowly, I clicked. My twin, as usual, had popped in with a hammer.

Doc's brown eyes, noticeably not silver like my Mom's, Mica's, or my own, squinted slightly at Mica before looking my way.

"Yes, well," my mom said with a big smile meant to smooth over the sarcasm, not at all hidden in Mica's tone, "it's been a busy summer for us all. I don't know how these kids manage to put in so many hours of practice fueled on French fries."

She and Gram shared a laugh that did little to break up the tension.

"I keep telling them French fries won't do it," Gram said, "but at least they have fish and vegetables tonight." Gram had always modeled healthy eating to support her athletic requirements. I'd never even seen her eat dessert. She was encouraging though, not judgmental. I respected her for it, even if I didn't always do what she said.

"Yes, indeed," Doc continued. "How have you been faring, Cami? Gotten all caught up on your training?" Doc asked.

Sensing my nervousness, Blake put his hand on my thigh under the table. The gesture, which usually got my blood pressure going up, succeeded in calming me down.

"Yes, sir," Blake answered for me, in his quiet deep voice that was so low it forced everyone to listen. "Cami and I have started to train together a bit more this summer. We've even managed to catch some dolphin swims, which makes a really intense workout."

My mouth dropped open, as did almost everyone's at the table. That wasn't something I'd planned to share. It appeared to shock everyone—except Doc, who nodded in a way that seemed like he was confirming information he already suspected.

How did I not know this? Why the hell haven't you brought me along? Mica screamed into my head.

How did he not know it? That was a good question, one I'd never pondered before about the what, where, and when of the information we shared via our private link.

Like you share everything with me lately? I tossed back at him.

"Doesn't everyone swim with dolphins?" Helix asked in a bored voice. "They're pretty much always around."

"Yes, but training with them is something very different," Doc said with a pointed look at his son. "Something few are able to do."

Helix rolled his eyes defensively, but quickly lowered them to his plate as if his peas held the answers to all the questions in the universe. I felt bad for him, and wondered how it would be if I were the one not swimming, not doing what everyone obsessed over around here.

"That's not safe, Cami!" Mom said; worry drawing the color from her usually tan cheeks.

"The dolphins have often trained our very best, Lydia," Doc said to my mom, earning a touch of my gratitude. "It's always a good thing."

"But things are different now," my mom stuttered, arguing with Doc, something I'd never seen her do.

This time, she got the evil eye from him and Gram and stayed silent for the rest of dinner. Mica   peppered Doc with questions about what kind of comas the kids were in, if he had found any similar cases elsewhere in the world, and what kinds of medications they were using to treat them.

Doc answered, patiently, making me wonder if our suspicions were completely unfounded. He gave information where he could and cited medical privacy laws where he couldn't. I couldn't tell whom he was trying to make feel better: Mica, my mom, or himself. It was obvious from the conversation, that he was actually concerned and working on this, no longer considering this a coincidence or no big deal.

See? I sent Mica. *He's doing everything he can.*

Maybe he is now, he conceded silently. *But, I still say he's hiding something. We need to get into that old lab.*

eleven

THE DAY OF the Surf Carnival AmPro, the actual traditional surfing contest felt like the pinnacle of summer, which, indeed, it was. It was the yearly kickoff to the Fourth of July weekend. Eighty degrees of sunny perfection capped with a wind that tickled my face and kicked up ten-foot swells that started deep. It was a glorious day for surfing, and it felt like the ocean was giving its support to the event.

There had been a great deal of talk about canceling, since it was so soon after the other deaths. Long debates with the Coast Guard, Surf Rescue organizations up and down the coast, and the other lifeguarding teams had resulted in some new regulations for the length of the heats, the number of extra guards, and equipment in the water. Plus, some cool new arm candy. Red and white plastic bracelets, complete with the lifeguarding seal, adorned the wrists of all contestants. They had RFID tags that could be activated quickly to search for any missing parties.

I admired the bracelet on my wrist, thinking I'd keep it on even after competition. Mica hated it; he said it threw shade on The Guard by drawing attention to the drownings. The Elders had argued against it too because they hated the idea of using modern technology part of our responsibility. "But, since the Surf Carnival hadn't been canceled since its inception, the bracelets were better than causing widespread panic and losing face, both of which would have happened if they'd called the whole thing off.

Billy had been pulling double duty lately with hours in the hospital for his residency and at long meetings with The Guard. The recent tragedies proved more than ever, that new blood was needed. They were willing to do anything to keep the Surf Carnival going. Some of the Elders, including Gramps, disagreed, saying The Guard test was really only one contest, closed to the public and held at the end of the summer. The Surf Carnival could be shut down so we had enough time to focus on the issues.

I agreed with him but probably just because I felt all buzzy today, and not in that exciting way that helped win competitions. Perhaps I'd stayed up too late the night before, catching up with Mica, but it was worth it.

I spent the most of last night with Alysha and Andrew at the hospital. Andrew had decided to surf today, because he thought Darwen would want him to, and I agreed. Alysha was inconsolable. She cried in a way she hadn't since the first week, finally admitting her fear Shayla would never wake up.

Her unhappy sobs haunted me at home, layering in with Mica's nerves about the surf competition. Thinking of how gutted Alysha was about Shay, I crept into Mica's room so we could have an actual conversation, instead of the casual chatter inside our heads. I brought my own beanbag chair, the one with my name on it that matched his, and we settled in like we used to when we were little.

I apologized for stealing his best friend, and he admitted my dating Blake wasn't the reason for his frequent ferry trips.

Jonas—the guy Blake had punched—was extremely close to getting sponsored for surfing. While our Island was known for our swimmers, and our ability to hold our own in the events at the Surf Carnivals, we'd yet to produce a professional surfer. Hanging out with Jonas, got Mica that much closer to a dream I didn't even know he had. Instead of letting me feel bad, he admitted he kept it from me on purpose so I didn't talk him out of giving up swim team, when school started again in the fall.

"The chlorine from the pools is making me crazy. Seriously, I can't do it anymore."

"But, you have state records! Not to mention, an invitation to try out for the national team."

"The gold medals are Blake's dream, not mine. I just like to race and win," he said, begging me with his eyes to understand. "The idea of spending all those hours training makes me want to cut off an arm, so I can't even compete."

"That probably wouldn't work," I joked, thinking of the intense pressure on Mica and Blake. Their times were inching on world records, whereas I was just one of the best swimmers in the state. I wasn't trying to put down my skills, but there was a difference.

"I can't do it," he said, shaking his head. "But I love surfing, and I figure, if I can come off tomorrow with some attention, I can get everyone off my back."

After Mica shared his secrets, I felt more comfortable sharing mine: how worried I was about this thing with

Blake causing problems between the three of us and, how scared I felt about falling in love with someone on-Island, how it felt like a trap.

To his credit, he didn't laugh at me or give me a hard time. Once I let him in on my feelings, he convinced me that whatever Blake and I had going was a good thing.

"Clearly the dolphins think so," he joked. "Because they picked you two to swim with, right?" I nodded, apologizing for not telling him about that right away or inviting him along for the ride. "I'm not sure it's your call," he said just before falling asleep at dawn. "But if you can swing it, I'd love to give it a try."

I GOT TO the beach way too early for the competition. I loved being the first one to ruin the tracks the sand Zamboni left behind. I hoped that watching the other competitors come in would help relax me. I hadn't really considered this was our biggest event, from a logistics point of view. The camera crews were there again, along with professional surfers and the brands that sponsored them.

Usually, there were three separate competitions: Junior heats, which I had placed high in last year, the Amateur, and the Elite/Professional. I watched the other competitors on the beach, and was caught off guard when unfamiliar hands reached around me from behind and covered my eyes.

"Ian!" I said, spinning to say hi to him, getting out of his grip. "Where's the camera?" I asked, looking around.

"Today, I'm in the competition, not on the crew. I heard your brother's the one to beat. Is that rumor true?" I nodded proudly.

My early start on the beach had helped, until the sand filled with competitors and fans. Mica was a jumble of performance anxiety and divided loyalty that did little to disperse the newly created tension between Blake and Jonas's friends. You'd think that negative energy, specific to a small group of people, could get lost in a crowd of hundreds, but it didn't. It seemed everyone was a bit on edge.

Even Ian knew about the Jonas/Blake tussle. "I heard your boyfriend's going out for boxing if this whole swimming thing doesn't work out," he teased, glancing over at Blake who was by the water doing his pre-game prep routine. I just laughed, until I noticed something on his wrist. Right next to the contest bracelet was one of Alysha's creations he'd bought at the Ocean Swim.

"Nice," I said, looking through the crowd to see if Alysha was around. "It would make her very happy to see that there."

He nodded. "Yeah, I've had a hard time reaching her. I've got about two hundred orders through my site, though. I was hoping to catch up with her today to talk about stocking them on IIWII permanently."

My eyes bugged out. "Wow! I didn't know models got to make those kinds of decisions," I said, meaning every word of it.

"Well, I sort of own the company," he said sheepishly. "I'm only the model, because it was the best way to ramp up publicity."

"That's going to mean a lot to her," I said, leaning up and giving him a hug. "Good luck today. I hope you, and Mica, and Blake can all get top spots."

The boys went first, twenty in a heat. The waves swelled high and deep—perfect for a contest like this because, there was plenty of room to ride them. It made it hard to see the contestants, though, and I hoped the judges were having better luck than I was. Mica, Blake, Ian, and Jonas had all won their heats and were competing in the final, with six other contestants.

Blake busted past the other surfers—one long ride, full of tricks I'd never seen him pull off in such quick succession. I couldn't take my eyes off of him.

When I went back to look for Mica, he wasn't there. And, he wasn't in my brain. The beach exploded with activity, and seemingly seconds later a lifeguard I didn't know was dragging me to the helicopter, so I could ride to the hospital with Mica.

twelve

THE CLICKS WERE gone. For the first time in my entire life,
the thoughts in my head were mine and mine alone. Mica
and I had shared silent communication even before we
knew words. For most of our lives, it was ideas, images,
and feelings between us. Only in the past few years, had
we gotten good at filtering. I'd learned to ignore every
single thought and feeling that came through from Mica.

Now, I'd give anything for even the slightest flicker.
But there wasn't a single blip. Not when I cradled him in
my arms for the endless minutes it took for the ambulance
to arrive at the beach, nor during the ride to hospital; or
when they spent unhelpful ages doing the same basic tests
that hadn't helped the others, at all. Since Mica had been
surfing, they spent a lot of time examining his head for
external bumps and bruises, which infuriated me to no
end.

"It's not from surfing!" I screamed at Billy, so loudly
he ordered me out of Mica's room. I stomped down the
hallway, hating the fake cheery blue walls and every single
person who came by, offering support. The only person I
needed right now was lying still and silent on a sick bed.
And, there was nothing I could do about it.

Billy came from the room, apologetic. "Cami, I know you're upset, and I want you to stay, but if you can't be calm, you have to leave. I can give you something to help, if you want."

"What, like a sedative?" I snorted, rolling my eyes.

Billy nodded, pity in his face. "Look, I gotta get back in to help Mica. Where's Blake? Can he sit here with you until your mom comes?"

My anger exploded. "I don't want him anywhere near me. This is all his fault!" I growled.

"What did Blake have to do with this?" Billy asked.

"He cut him off!" I wailed. "Because he wanted to win. He didn't even notice when Mica went down—he just kept going! Because winning was so damn important, nothing else mattered."

Billy's eyes widened even further and he patted my shoulder awkwardly.

"Cami, Blake didn't do this," he said.

"Then why are you looking for bumps on Mica's head?" I sobbed out.

"It's a precaution," Billy said, using an extremely gentle voice. "We wouldn't be doing our job if we didn't. But you and I both know this looks just like the others."

"What if it's not? What if it's worse?" I asked.

"I won't let that happen, Cami," Billy said, his voice choking on the words. "Not to Mica. I need to get back in there. So, can you stay here and stay calm?"

"I've got her," Celeste said, putting a hand on my shoulder and leaned in to give Billy a kiss. His eyes got teary from her kindness, and I felt awful for yelling at him. Mica belonged to him, almost as much as he belonged to me. So, I didn't begrudge the extra seconds he stayed in the hug before going back to Mica's room to save him for me.

With her full concentration and sympathy on me, I collapsed into Celeste's arms. Within seconds, I'd soaked her shirt with tears. She didn't care; she just let me cry until I'd drained every tear for the moment.

"Thanks for skipping the 'it's all going to be okay' speech," I said, sniffling in gratitude. She hadn't interrupted, even once, with any of the ridiculous chatter I'd said to Alysha when she'd been in this very same position.

Of course, then it had seemed like a random accident, whereas now it seemed like something was very, very wrong.

By the time Blake arrived, my fight had left. Even lifting my eyes to look at him felt like too much work. I needed every bit of strength to ignore the way my heart beat a little faster the second he walked in.

"I'm sorry I didn't get here sooner," he said, leaning in to hug me, "but I had to wait to talk to The Guard."

"Why? To get your trophy?" I asked, anger oozing with the words. He froze mid-reach for me.

"No," he said, shocked at my outburst, "they needed statements. To try and figure out what happened."

"I'm going to give you guys a minute," Celeste said, attempting to rise from her spot at my side.

"Stay," I gripped her arm. She settled back on the bench, clearly uncomfortable. But, at that moment, I needed her, and, selfishly, I just didn't care that I was putting her in an uncomfortable position.

"You go," I said to Blake. "Now!" Blake's eyes flashed, golden flecks of fire coming through the silver as he prepared to argue, but I wasn't about to let him get a word in. "I told you at the beach I didn't want to see you. Were you too happy about your win to listen to me?"

"Cami, I didn't win. They called the contest," Blake sighed wearily. "Why are we even talking about this? What's going on with Mica?"

"Nothing. Nothing is going on with him. He's flat on a bed, in a coma. Thanks to you."

"What does this have to do with me?" Blake asked, heating red under his golden skin. He bristled with strength and anger I'd never felt directed at me before. "I had no idea what was happening. You know I would have helped if I had."

With a couple deep breaths through his nose, he calmed visibly, quickly changing tactics, attempting again to touch me. My body responded defiantly. It wanted his comfort, but my brain didn't agree. I jerked my arm from his reach as if it were a jellyfish sting.

"Just go," I whispered, turning my face back into Celeste's shirt, hoping he'd listen.

But, he didn't, so I ignored him. With every minute he remained, it got harder to fight the urge to go to him. I wanted to go back to the days where there had been absolutely zero attraction and I'd avoided physical contact with him. Mica's condition felt like a punishment for finding time for my love life when, clearly, every spare moment should have been dedicated to helping Shay and Darwen.

In hiccoughed whispers, I tried to explain to Celeste, who patiently tried to talk me out of my sudden anxiety. "Just give yourself time to calm down," Celeste soothed. I felt comforted by her voice, even though I didn't believe her words.

I took a peek at Blake, standing tight-lipped in the corner, attempting to respect my wishes, but clearly not wanting to leave. Though he wore headphones and tapped his long fingers angrily on the same board shorts he'd worn in the competition, I still felt him listening. Feeling evil, wanting him to feel my pain, I sent dagger eyes at him to pierce his golden-boy cool.

Immediately, Blake silently slipped out of the exit and down the fire stairs, setting off the alarm in his haste. The jaw-breaking noise sliced though my ears, straight to my gut like a spike. Loud enough to wake the dead, I prayed for it to wake the comatose, instead.

"Mica would never be mad at anyone for playing to win; least of all Blake," Alysha said in a quiet voice. In the three weeks since Shayla' accident, Alysha's sparkle had dimmed.

"I know, but I think…" I paused and swallowed. "That somehow the trouble started when Blake and I got together. So, maybe I need to stay away to make it better."

"I could slap you right now," Alysha said, carefully digging her chipping black fingernails into her palms. My eyes opened wide in surprise at the anger coming from my least intense friend. "Blake helped you when you got hurt. Did it occur to you that he saved you from the same thing?" She paused, but instead of letting me answer, she held a finger up to my lips. I shook my head, but her rant had just begun. "Seeing you with him is the only thing that's given me any hope this summer. You just shine when he's around—you actually look whole again in a way that you haven't since Kaleb left. You guys are right. Want to fix things? Figure out why the three of them aren't alive or dead, but in some strange sleep. Why have twenty-five more dolphins stranded this week? Don't throw away the only thing about this summer that isn't wrong."

Iysha's lecture helped to diffuse my anger at Blake, but it got me thinking horrible things about my mother. As hospital administrator, she should have solved this problem for Darwen and Shay before this ever happened to Mica. Then, Gram walked in and took me into Mica's room.

"This is her very worst nightmare come true," Gram said, disappointment etching even more lines in her sun-weathered face. "She has done everything she could do for you your entire lives, to keep you healthy and safe. The last thing she needs to feel from you is that she isn't doing enough."

Gram didn't usually play the blame game. It was shocking to hear her so angry—but she was right, and that was exactly why I was so upset.

"But, Mom didn't do anything this time, Gram. We all did nothing. Just went on about our lives."

"This is no more her fault than it is yours. She and Doc have been trying everything they can think of."

"Everything that they can do here. What about the Mainland hospital?"

"Just because they haven't shared every decision with you, doesn't mean they haven't considered it all, Cami," she said, tight-lipped. "You have to know that. But, certain things raise more questions than we want to answer."

I took a breath, wanting her to take me seriously. "So why haven't they gotten more help?" I asked, frustrated.

She looked down. But, not before I saw the tear in the corner of her eye. In all our years, I'd never seen Gram this upset.

"I'm sorry," I said, taking her hand. I was doing the same thing to her as I'd done to my Mom, to Blake: pushing away those that were there for me. It helped to keep a lid on the rage I felt toward all those who weren't here, when they should have been. Like Kaleb, and my dad. I knew my anger wasn't helping Mica, and it made me feel awful. I took a deep breath and gave Gram a hug. "I respect the old ways," I told her, "I really do—but this has never happened before. Don't you think something new needs to be done? Or, at least, tried?"

Gram looked at me, "I do."

I felt triumphant. Even so, Gram put up her hand to stop me from even mentally celebrating.

"Consider this, Cami," she said, gravely. "Those tests are Xrays and radiation. If you're still concerned that sonar might have had something to do with the comas, then the tests could be dangerous for Mica. Are you prepared to take that risk?"

I nodded, without hesitation. "We have to. Don't you see? If we don't try something new, then we can't learn anything we don't already know."

She nodded, her eyes shifting around the room to check out the various pieces of medical equipment tethered to Mica.

"I'll speak to your mother. If she insists on more testing, then the Doc will do it. But, you need to be nicer to her. Deal?"

I nodded, hoping she could convince her, and praying that the test wouldn't do any further harm to Mica. My mom and Gram had often been at odds during my life. If Gram was working this hard to protect my mother, then I needed to listen.

"Come, sit," Gram said, pulling an extra chair to the spot by the bed where my mother sat next to Mica, holding his hand. I gave my mom a silent hug and she hugged me back—without ever letting go of Mica's hand.

The few monitors in the room were silent and steady, and for a moment all I heard was the wooshing in and out of Mica's breath. I was so grateful for every single one.

We sat in silence together, Gram holding my hand and Mom's, Mom holding Mica's hand and Gram's, linking us in a chain. It made me think.

"Come, let's give your mom some time," Gram said, leading me from the room. We sat in the hallway, which had become way too familiar to me lately.

"Did Gramps tell you we talked to Stoney and him about the ears and stuff that ran common in our people?" I asked. She looked at me quickly, nodding but not quite meeting my eyes. She shifted back to looking at Mica, so I looked at him too. Laid out flat on the hospital bed, his usually frantic energy was only relayed in bleeps and flashes on the equipment. I vowed right then to do absolutely anything to get him back to normal as soon as possible.

I continued, "Don't you think it's kind of strange that in your generation the hereditary traits are split up a bit, but in mine we all have them?" She looked at me, meeting my gaze this time. "I'm beginning to think we didn't all just get super lucky with the hand we drew from the possible combinations of DNA."

"I suppose anything's possible," she said. "The gods work in mysterious ways."

"We're not exactly heaven sent," I said. Gaining my nerve, I went on, "Gram, what's in the old lab?"

Gram's eyes widened, but she responded smoothly. "That old lab is just that—old. Leave it, Cami. It's been closed for years."

"Why, Gram?" I asked quietly, careful to tread lightly on such delicate ground.

"Because Doc was making the Elders all nervous, messing with nature. We stopped the treatments, shut it down."

I paused, taking in the information, not wanting to alert Gram that she just told me something I never heard before.

"What if there's some information down there that could help? Tests and stuff?"

"Everything we need has been taken out, and it's been sealed for years. There's nothing down there that could help us, and you can't get in, anyway."

I nodded, but I began to plan.

thirteen

"BRUCELLOCIS," I READ. "What is that?"

Helix and I were in my bedroom reading over files he had uncovered and printed, earlier that day. Since I'd stopped training for personal reasons, he helped me when he wasn't at the snack bar. I wouldn't say we'd become friends, exactly, but we had a good working relationship. I finally asked him why he agreed to help with all of this.

"I want to study painting, and my dad is adamantly refusing to pay for college, unless I go for science of some kind. He's given up on me being a doctor, but he wants me working on some kind of 'ology.' I'm not him, but he doesn't see it that way." I nodded, understanding all too well about family expectations.

After telling me about his dream to study painting, he became shy again, turning back to the marine biology we were trying to understand at the moment. "Brucellocis. It's a dolphin disease," he read. "An infection that can . . ." Squinting, he stopped to click a link, and then muttered quietly, "that can cause infertility in dolphins."

"I knew I'd heard that word before!" I exclaimed, grabbing the iPad of his hands to search my bookmarks for one of the thousands of articles I'd saved in the past week.

Unfortunately, I was gathering information too quickly to even remember what I read.

"This," I said, finally showing him an article that talked about an increase of the disease in dolphins in the Gulf of Mexico, since the oil spill in 2010.

"'Ten times the dead dolphins as usual,'" Helix read, "'including calves and unborn fetuses.' But what, exactly, is the disease?"

"And, do you think it's around here?" I asked, getting excited. This could be something.

Helix looked back and forth between his dad's notes and the article, comparing the two.

"I don't know about now," he said, so slowly I was ready to scream. "But, I think that it was. We need Billy for this."

I knew Billy was home; I saw him hanging on his family's dock, fishing with Blake. So, it went without saying that if we needed Billy, I wasn't going to get one without the other.

"Nah," I said, "this is about the dolphins. Let's call Celeste."

Celeste came over quickly, helping us understand the notes, and she explained details about the disease. It matched details of what was happening around the Island in the years before we were born.

"This was his working hypothesis, it seems," Celeste confirmed. Looking more closely at the medical jargon in the notes, she confirmed that the condition at the time was undetected in both patients and dolphins alike. Instead of calling attention to the matter, Doc had begun treating on-

Island women as part of his fertility treatment. First, he ordered any woman who wanted to get pregnant to trade fish consumption for vegetables.

"You guys eat a ton of fish, just like the dolphins do. If this was coming from food they ate, then it was likely in the food your parents were eating, too."

"If people were sick from eating fish, why didn't they know it?" He asked, posing the question we were all thinking.

"It could have been a build-up over years," Celeste said. "They wouldn't necessarily have felt anything. And, it was just a hypothesis, so your dad probably didn't want to say anything in case he was wrong."

"So he was hiding something, even back then," I said.

"Not exactly, sweetie," Celeste said, running a patient hand over my hair. I appreciated her comfort in the moment. "In an active study, second-guessing his experiments in public wouldn't have helped. And, in this case, it does seem that some of these measures worked." She looked at the file again, before continuing. "In addition to cutting fish consumption, Doc administered an intense course of antibiotics from the time women began his treatments through their pregnancy. The injections had been nothing more than strong-scale antibiotics meant to keep the Brucellosis, at bay so the unborn babies could stay viable."

"So, that was it? His whole big fertility secret was penicillin?" I asked, incredulous that the guy we were expected to treat like a god, acted as little more than a pharmacist.

"I don't think so," Helix said, "because it doesn't really explain all the twins."

I nodded, and Celeste did, too.

"So," I gulped, ready to ask the million-dollar question and afraid of what the answer would be. "Do you think this is what's going on right now?"

"I'm pretty sure the tests for this disease were part of the course of tests Doc did right after Shay went down," Celeste said, "though I'll double-check. But, if this was the answer, Shay and Mica would already be fine."

"How?" I asked, drooping under the weight of a failing step forward.

"They've had antibiotics," Helix answered. "Plenty of them, and they still haven't woken up."

I took in the news; it hurt my heart. Helix awkwardly patted my shoulder, while Celeste scooped me up in a hug and let me cry for the hundredth time that week. When my most recent bout of tears was spent, I looked at the two of them and strengthened my resolve.

"So, this is just the first part of his process?" I asked.

Helix nodded. "This was all the information we had at home."

I nodded. I think I knew where to find the rest.

The water had only been closed for a day after Mica. His condition had been classified under head injury. I found myself nefariously hoping for someone else to go down, so maybe they would take it seriously.

Blake hadn't stopped though. Every morning, he waited outside my house for me, board in hand, expecting me to gosurfing. I wouldn't, but he persisted.

The first two days, I ignored him. The second two, I slammed the front door. Yesterday, when he had the audacity to, once again, turn up with a surfboard, I gave in to my own needs and cursed him out.

"Are you crazy?" I screeched, pleased when his eyes went wide Yelling made me feel mentally closer to Mica, which, of course, Blake saw right through.

"Screaming won't make him better," Blake said slowly, the quiet vibration of his tone reaching into a part of me that I quickly slapped down. "But, surfing might. Make you feel better, I mean; closer to him."

"Surfing? With you? That's what got him into this mess!" I used all of my mental armor to not react to the pain that appeared in his eyes when I threw out the words like daggers.

"Cami, he's my best friend. I would never..." he struggled to get the words out. "You know that! I can't even..." He whirled around, like an animal himself. "God! What you're saying!" He shook his head. "It's making me sick."

I could see it was. He looked horrified, and haunted, and so alone. But I couldn't—I wouldn't—be the person to make him feel better.

"Not as sick as Mica, though," I jabbed. "And even if he could go, he wouldn't go with you."

In truth, the thought of surfing, of letting the waves calm my pain for just a little while, was exactly what I wanted to do. Mica would definitely have escaped to the waves and let them work their magic on his mood.

"You're wrong," Blake said. "You can think want you want about what happened out there, make me the one to blame. But Mica? He'd be the first one to tell you that you're way off base here, and I think you know that."

"No, I really don't," I snapped quickly.

"No. The problem is that you're placing blame on everyone. And at the moment, it's me, which is ridiculous," he said, finally losing the steady calm that was so not working on me, anyway.

Good! I was mad, and sad; and I wanted him to be, too. It killed me that, even though I hadn't said it out loud, he knew it, and threw it right back at me.

"Cami, these past few weeks with you, they've been beyond amazing. If you don't want to be with me that way anymore, I'll accept it. And, since I know we've got other things to worry about, I won't even ask you why right now. But us not being together, even as friends? How can you live with that?"

"Aren't you the one who said life, right now, is nothing like normal? Even if you didn't cause what happened to Mica—and I said if—the fact you want to go surfing, instead of spending every possible second trying to find out why this is happening, and how we can fix it, is absolute proof you have no clue."

"None of us do, not even Doc. Not for a second, have I stopped thinking about Mica or Shay or Darwen. It kills me that I don't know how to help them. And that whatever's happened to them, could happen to me—or you—next. All I know is that my best friend is in a coma right now and I could be next. So, I'll be damned if I'm going to spend more useless hours locked up in a room researching science and theories I don't understand."

"So, just chuck it all, grab a board and go? And if you go down, okay, 'cuz at least you were surfing? You can live with that?"

"Yeah. I can. If the same thing happens to you, you'll have wasted these days alone, crying and sitting inside, frantically searching a computer for answers that clearly aren't there. Instead, you could be with me. Outside, doing something we love."

My jaw dropped, and then the tears fell down my cheeks, pushed out of my eyes by the horrible truth of what he was saying. My armor had been shattered. He was talking about how to spend his last days—his last minutes—and that he wanted them to be with me.

He approached me; I let him.

"Doesn't being with me on the waves sound better than how you spent yesterday?" he asked, wiping my tears away with the pads of his thumbs, cradling my face in his sun-warmed hands.

For all of two seconds I sunk into his touch, and into the idea that Blake and I together was right, not wrong, that our being together could make this better, instead of worse. My heart slowed and I closed my eyes, hearing all the sounds around me: the birds and waves, the splashing of water on the dock, the chirp of the dolphins, somewhere in the distance. Avoiding Blake was about more than my love life; it was about everything.

I opened my eyes again, facing reality. "It's not that simple, Blake. This is up to me. I don't know why, or how,

I am supposed to do this, but I know it is. Pretending that surfing will solve our problems hasn't worked so far. We need science and facts, not dolphins and waves. As long as Mica is lying down, instead of standing here next to us, waxing his board to go surfing, I can't even stomach the thought of going myself. Or, being around anyone who can."

fourteen

IT FELT LIKE midnight, considering the town was eerily quiet, but it was only nine and barely dark. The drama had definitely kept some of the tourists away. Usually, people stayed until the beach closed at dusk, stopping in town before going home. A full moon illuminated the emptiness. The few tourists around seemed aware they missed the party, but didn't know why.

Taking advantage of the emptiness, Darwen's twin, Andrew, and I walked over to the snack bar where Alysha and Helix were the only ones working. I'd told them about the lab in the lighthouse after I'd gone back a second time to see if it was possible to break in.

I needed Helix to figure out how to disengage the alarm. We already ransacked his dad's office and found information on the make and model number of the alarm. Creepy online chat boards about breaking and entering gave out codes and instructions that Helix understood.

He was generous with his help on the ground, but adamantly refused to get in the water with me. And I needed someone to help me get in so I asked Andrew, figuring he had as much at stake as I did. He wanted to help in theory, but wasn't easily convinced. "What is so important that it's locked up underwater and secret?" Andrew asked.

I couldn't really help.

"Even if it can't help Mica, Darwen and Shay, there's a reason The Guard built that lab to begin with, then closed it down, and kept it hidden all these years. We need to find out what it is."

"But it's breaking and entering, Cami. Big time," Andrew said, looking worried.

"Do you know how many laws we've already broken?" I asked. Angry sparks of feeling popped up on my skin. The same feeling I had the day of the surfing contest when I knew something important was in the air. That day I hadn't understood the warning, today I did. Our answers were in that lab. I knew it but I had no proof. And Andrew couldn't be talked into going on just my instincts.

Even Helix started to turn.

"Going through files in my house is not the same, and you know it," Helix said.

But, I didn't really; currently public law didn't guide my moral compass. I had three definite points that mattered most: Mica, Shay, and Darwen—all down for the count. For them, I would do absolutely anything I needed to, but I had to convince the others that my personal sense of right and wrong mattered most.

"You know what's wrong? A whole town sitting quietly while people get hurt; a whole town willing to keep truths buried under the sea," I argued.

"What exactly do you expect to find?" Helix asked, wearily.

"More about the injections and the individual project notes," I said, hoping that would convince him. The general data from the fertility experiment helped us understand the steps Doc had taken in his plans, but not why or how, exactly. We needed to know more in order to be able to help the others, because with every day that passed, their chances for coming out of the comas got worse.

"I'll think about it," said Andrew.

Alysha and Helix closed down the snack bar at the end of their shift. It had been so slow all night they had the wood panels up and the locks in place only five minutes after close.

"I'll walk you home," Andrew offered, ignorant of the daggers aimed at his head. If Alysha had any indication of Helix's interest, she didn't act like it.

He stayed on the pier with me as I did my best to talk him into it.

"Helix," I said, putting my hand on his arm, "this isn't a burglary, really. These records are our history. We all need to know what they say about us, or we won't have any kind of a future."

He stared at me long and hard, conflict apparent in his eyes. They were brown, unlike Blake's or mine. My words sounded manipulative, but I believed them with all my heart. One look told me, it wasn't enough to convince him.

My eyes filled; fear and concern spilled down my cheeks. I'd always hated girls who turned on the tears to get what they wanted. But, I was genuinely overcome with emotion. Admittedly, I felt gratified when the waterworks changed the conversational tide. Helix grabbed me and held on as I sobbed, his unfamiliar frame reinforcing just how alone I was. The person comforting me was someone I had barely spoken to before this crazy summer began. When he whispered he was sorry for making me cry, and he would do whatever I wanted, I felt embarrassing gratitude for whatever force in the universe it was that made boys cave when girls cried.

Of course, not two seconds later, I cursed that same force when I heard a familiar voice behind me.

"So, is this why you broke up with me?" Blake grumbled. "I thought maybe it was that Ian guy from TV."

Still sniveling, I lifted my head off of Helix's now-wet shoulder and turned to face Blake. He had that look, the scary one I had seen when he'd punched the surfer on the Mainland beach. With every molecule in my body, I knew he wouldn't hurt me. But, I wasn't so sure about Helix, who Blake out-muscled by at least forty pounds.

I stepped between them and did the only thing I could think of right then; I turned the tears back on. The sad was never very far away lately, so it was way too easy. Even though I wasn't faking, exactly, I felt guilty for the emotional manipulation.

I also felt grateful because, once again, it worked. Blake backed up, diffused and distracted, as intended. His face quickly moved through a spectrum of human emotion: anger, embarrassment, and sadness.

"If he is—this is—what you want . . . or need . . . then . . ." he stuttered, backing up even further. My heart dropped.

"Helix and me?" I asked, incredulous.

"Well, yeah. You won't hang out with me at all. I know he was in your room the other day. And then I find you here, like this."

On my other side, I could feel Helix's shock. His head shook 'no' while his body quaked with fear. For all of five seconds, I considered taking the bait Blake had cast.

Helix could be a good cover to keep Blake away, but, the histrionics I'd orchestrated in just the past few minutes already weighed me down. There was no way I could lie about a whole relationship. Only honestly would get us all off the hook. But I made Blake squirm a little, while I debated how much of the truth I wanted to share.

"As you may or may not realize, I have a few other things on my mind besides boys and dating."

"So you've mentioned. A few hundred times," Blake said.

"We were talking about the lighthouse," Helix said, "and how crazy it would be to break in."

"You're actually considering this?" Blake asked, directing his question to me.

"Did you, or did you not, tell me to go out in the world to get the answers I need?" I said.

"That is not what I meant," Blake said, tossing up his hands in frustration.

"Well, sorry if I don't exactly have time for the complex interpretation of your word choice while my brother wastes away in a hospital bed."

Blake rolled his eyes, channeling one of Mica's common expressions as much as my out-of-character sarcasm channeled my twin's frequent tone.

"Ignoring the law for a second, how do you plan to get around the swimming ban?"

"Leave from my dock," I said, shrugging, "and stay out of sight. I went again on my own, but didn't set off the alarm."

"Yeah, but as soon as you touch the door, that will happen again," Blake said.

I glanced at Helix, unsure how much to say about his role in this plan. Luckily, he decided for me.

"That's my job," Helix said softly, "I'm going to turn off the alarm, before she even goes in."

"Can you do that?" Blake asked, his voice filled with awe as he included Helix in the conversation for the first time.

"I think so. It's certainly possible, according to the schematics."

"And then what?" Blake asked. "You sneak in from the ocean and nobody has to know?"

I nodded. It was as far as we'd gotten on the rest of the plan.

"What about the water getting in from the door? Or the files getting all wet when you swim them out?"

"There's a double door in place," Helix said. "If she's quick to close the first one, only a couple feet of water will get in. It'll basically be a bit of a wet floor in the main room."

"A bit of wet floor? You guys are crazy if you really think that's all you're going to have to deal with down there."

"Well, I guess I'll have to have something waterproof to put stuff in so I can take it out," I said, thinking out loud about some issues we had yet to consider, "and a camera to make sure I can photograph anything too big to carry."

"That's what you're worried about? That's downright nuts. What if something happens to you?"

"Then I'll get arrested," I shrugged. "At least we'd have something to show to make the Island send someone back in."

"That's the best-case scenario, as I see it," Blake said, frustrated. "What if you get hurt? What if you go down?"

"Then, at least I go down fighting. You wanted to do this too when we first found the lab. So why give me a hard time now?"

"Because it's dangerous! For you! And you're so consumed with what you want you're not thinking it through."

"I will," I growled. "You just go back to surfing, and I'll get it done."

"Not without me, you won't," he argued, holding up a hand without letting me get in the next word. "I get that you don't want me around—even if, for the life of me, I can't understand why. But, you will have me for this. There is no way I'm letting you do it alone."

"You're not in charge of me, Blake. It's not your call."

"Then it better be yours," he growled, turning his attention back to Helix. "If. You. Do. Not. Call. Me," Blake said, crowding Helix towards the edge of the dock, "You will not live to regret it. Got it?"

Blake backed off when Helix nodded, and headed off down the pier. Helix stared at me, a million questions all over his face.

"He has nothing to do with this," I said, before he could ask. "You worry about the alarm, and I'll take care of the rest, including Blake."

A day later, I ignored Blake's fierce stares, in a hospital waiting room I'd never been in before. Billy's rented CAT scan machine had come in, and we'd convinced him to at least take a look at the rest of us. Blake was still pissed at me, more obviously than ever, but he traded his anger over the break-up, to anger over the break-in.

Luckily, he kept quiet about it in front of Celeste. She was on the island for her career, and we'd exposed her to enough trouble already.

"He wants answers just like you do," Celeste said. "Maybe more."

"Not possible, or he wouldn't have waited so long for these tests."

"MRIs and CAT scans have their dangers; they expose patients to radiation and can cause greater trauma in some cases. While I agree that Doc waited longer than he should have to replace the old machine, waiting a bit is understandable."

"Isn't this usually what happens for head injuries and comas?" Blake asked.

"Yes, normally, if you were in a big city and in a traditional hospital, but that's not what you are dealing with here. Many things that MRIs and CAT scans can rule out have been ruled out in these cases by other tests. It's a combination of factors."

"Still, Doc is hiding something. And, as far as I am concerned, if he knows anything that's not being used to help Mica and the others, then that completely cancels out every bit of help he's ever given."

"Let's just see if we find anything," Celeste said as Mica was wheeled in.

Mica came through the electronic tests with his vitals intact. Perhaps better than when he started, though that wasn't something I could exactly share.

For just a second when he was inside the MRI, I thought I felt a blip from him. Perhaps it was wishful thinking, but I swear I felt a searing pulse inside my head when he was in the machine. It only happened once, so I didn't say anything.

"Are you okay?" My mom asked. She nervously paced the room the entire time Mica was on the other side of the glass window. For an always-in-control hospital administrator, she seemed uncomfortably out of place here when her own son was being tested. .

I nodded, hoping to lose her attention so I could ponder the pulse. Was it random, or coming from Mica?

"Mom, is this hurting him?" I asked, after it happened again. Even the idea I had insisted on doing something that might cause him pain stabbed another hole in my heart.

"No, sweetie, he can't feel a thing," she said. "Why do you ask? Is it hurting you?" My mom had very little idea of what exactly went on between Mica and me. But, there had been many times through childhood where one of us fell down and the other cried. That was a common twin link, and it was something that was easy for her to understand.

"It was sweet when they were little," Mom explained to Celeste. "One of them would cry when the other got hurt, even if they weren't in the same room. Blake, do you remember when Mica fell on the dock with you, that Fourth of July when you were ten, or so?" Blake nodded and I did, too. "Cami was inside helping me," she continued. "She dropped to the floor, crying and holding her knee. There was nothing there I could see, but it wasn't more than a minute later that Blake carried Mica in, who wound up needing nine stitches on his knee. Isn't that amazing?" she asked, to herself or Celeste, I really couldn't tell. Celeste walked her over to the glass and put an arm around her shoulders, providing her a little bit of comfort on this truly uncomfortable day.

Blake, came over my way, stepping right up to whisper in my ear. The innocent contact fired up every nerve on that side of my body, reminding me how much I missed even his most casual touch.

"Did you feel something, or did he, like, say hello?" Blake asked.

Tears filled my eyes, but in this case, I wasn't trying to use them to play keep-a-way. I couldn't help it. It was bad enough there was silence in my head where Mica's thoughts used to be. Alysha and I had spoken about this at length, but Blake and I had not.

"Look, I'm not trying to upset you. I was just hoping," he shrugged.

"I felt something," I told him, "like a brain blip or something—but I don't think it's anything he said."

"Bio-sonar?" he asked, raising an eyebrow, echoing the thoughts I'd had in the car.

"It's a long shot, don't you think?" I asked, "Besides, Celeste would think I really was crazy then!"

"But, you're not, and we all know it. Screw the pact. Say something, at least to Billy. If you don't, then Doc's not the only one holding onto info that may help everyone out."

As I pondered Blake's suggestion, Doc and Billy came to our side of the room and the activity level jumped up a very big notch. Doc sat at the desk and began to manipulate the files on the computer screen. Suddenly, we saw the inside of Mica's brain.

"There are no trauma points," Doc said to my Mom, moving slightly to the side so she could take a look. "That's the good news."

"So, what's the bad?" she whispered. I gave her credit for her inquiry, because it was a question I was far too afraid to ask.

"His brain is bigger than normal," Doc replied, "and I can't tell if it's due to recent all-over swelling, or if it's just the way he was born." Figures. Hundreds of tests on our bodies throughout the years, and the one piece of information that was relevant for today had never been looked into before. "We can treat the swelling again, this time more directly," Doc said, "but it's risky. The medication is very invasive and may compromise his other working functions."

"You think it's the right thing to do?" Mom asked. Doc hemmed and hawed for a second, and shot a look at Billy, very obviously giving him permission to talk.

"I think there's a better way," Billy said, looking back and forth between my mother and me. "But, it involves Cami, and presents other risks."

"I'll do it. Anything," I said, not even giving them a chance to explain.

An hour later I was in the MRI machine. The column I lay on closed around me like the most terrifying wave, the kind that felt like it could push you under the sand. Claustrophobia set in, which I had never experienced before. In that way, the test was easier for Mica than me. Billy went over the risks with Mom and me at least five times, even after I'd agreed. Since Mica and I were only fraternal twins and not identical, the information gleaned from the tests would still be hypothetical at best.

Had it been Blake and Kaleb, he explained, the results would have been more reliable. Identical twins share exactly the same DNA. If their two brains were both larger than normal, then Billy would have the right information. He had calls in to Shayla and Darwen's parents to ask if Alysha and Andrew could come for their twin's scans. So, I went along.

Once the results were in, his guess proved right—my brain was the same size as Mica's. I also had similar inner ear damage, but that took a back seat, because nothing they'd done to address that theory had accomplished anything. Blake went next for the sake of further comparison. His brain size was the same as both Mica's and mine. Billy and Celeste were quite excited in an adorably shared, geeky way that had me longing to take Blake up on the comfort he'd offered the other day. As for me, I couldn't help but feel a bit disappointed.

"What were you expecting, Cami?" Billy asked, putting his arm around me in the hallway and walking me to a quiet corner, while we waited on Celeste and Blake to bring coffee. This wing of the hospital housed long-term care patients and had a different rhythm than emergency and intensive care. Patients went by on stretchers, pushed by unfamiliar-looking orderlies barking instructions at every person who walked by.

"I hoped we'd find something obvious; something clearly damaged and could be fixed," I said quietly. "Like a blood clot that you could drain, or something that would get him up right away."

"That's not usually how medicine works. But, there is also nothing obvious that indicates Mica will have any kind of long-term damage; there's no visible injury to his brain. This is important. You did good," he said, giving my shoulders a warm squeeze.

"So what happens now?"

"We do the test for the others; study the size of their brains."

"But what does any of it matter if it doesn't help Mica to wake up?"

"Just because it doesn't help right away, doesn't mean it won't help eventually. I thought you'd be happy with some confirmation that there was something unique, but also common, between you all. Isn't that what you've said all along?"

I nodded. "Do you think it's enough to get The Guard to force Doc to open his lab?"

"It's a start," Billy said. "If we can confirm with a few more of the twins, I think it will be impossible for them to say no. But let's just keep that quiet, okay? It's really important right now we still get Doc's help."

Alysha came over after I woke up from an avoid-everyone-and-everything nap. She redid my hair, shaving the sides even though my stitches were long gone. It seemed like the right thing to do, considering Mica had kept his up all summer. I had a bit of a scar that was obvious now and I liked it.

"It feels like forever ago, the first time we did this," I said to Alysha as she stood behind me. The mirror showed two friends who'd changed tremendously this summer.

"I know you're upset and I wish I could tell you it would get better, but it just sucks," Alysha said, smoothing in the ends of my hair as she French-braided it.

"Why are you so resigned all of a sudden? You did the CAT scan today with Shay?" I asked even though I already knew she had. "That was at least interesting news."

"I'm tired of arguing with everyone," she said, a huge tear rolling down her face. "It's not helping Shay, not helping my parents, and not helping me—and it's not helping you, either."

She'd been fighting her parents every day since Shay first went down. And, it was true that the last few times I'd talked to her about what was happening, she'd begged off the conversation, walked away, or simply hung up the phone. At the time, I let it go, because I thought that's what she needed. But, now that I was in the same position, I knew I had actually let her down by allowing her to pull away.

"I'm sorry I've been avoiding you," Alysha continued. "I couldn't handle the endless speculation and debate about what's happening. But now Mica is in a coma too, I couldn't just leave you here alone."

"Thanks," I said, nodding as if I understood when, really, I didn't at all. Perhaps, because it was so fresh to me, I didn't get her perspective. The longer Shay had been out, the more important it became to ask questions—at least, to me. Mica's absence—and the resulting silence in my head—only made me more desperate to get to the bottom of what was going on with my friends and the ocean.

I was so relieved when Alysha and her parents had agreed to the CAT. After what my test and Blake's revealed earlier in the day, Doc and Billy actually managed to persuade the hospital and Alysha and her parents it was urgent. If they had had time to think about it, I'm not sure they would have said yes.

"Can I ask you one thing?" I asked cautiously. I wasn't sure I could handle Alysha pulling away again. "Have you heard Shay at all since . . ."

She shook her head no before I even completed the sentence. "I thought . . . for a second, I thought I did: when she and I were getting our CAT scans today. But, it was nothing specific—I think it was more like interference from the machine."

"Or wishful thinking," I said, reaching back to grab her hand. "I thought the same thing."

"Yeah, Billy said it was part of the way the machine worked," she said. "And I promised my parents not to give Doc a hard time, so I didn't even bring it up. Can we drop it now, too? Please?"

I nodded and got up from the chair. From that moment on, I let her distract me with superficial matters. We cooked spaghetti, and made s'mores out back by the fire pit, eating them inside on the sofa while we watched HGTV.

The night felt so normal, I almost forgot the only reason we were alone, was because Shay and Mica were in the hospital.

Outside, the dolphins chirped, playing in the water near my house and making such a racket, it seemed they were inviting me out to play. I imagined stapling myself to the sofa, because my need to swim overwhelmed me. I craved the water and that element of play that my dolphin brought to me even in my worst nights. But, because Alysha was there, I couldn't go.

But the idea wouldn't leave. Pictures of me in the water repeated in my head over and over again, like that game Mica and I used to play when we wanted to drive each other crazy: the timeless sibling tradition of copying what the other says over and over again. The game inevitably ended in a draw when the copy-ee flipped things on the copy-er so both wind up repeating the same thing over and over again.

Mica and I had our own silent version of the game, which ended with pictures stuck in my head. Our sent images were meant to disturb, horrify, embarrass, or crack up, depending on the situation. While the image of me playing with my dolphin was inherently pleasing, having it on repeat when I couldn't go made me feel borderline insane.

Alysha stayed with me all night and most of the next day. It really complicated things since that night I planned to break in to the lab. It took every ounce of willpower not to let her in on my plan. I fully intended to share the results with her as soon as I had what I needed, but I was concerned she would talk me out of going. Luckily, she went to work in the early afternoon, so I had time to prepare and gather what I needed for the break in at the lab.

I borrowed one of Mica's weight belts and a few of his scuba diving hooks to attach to my wetsuit. I also grabbed some dry packs to put into a backpack for papers. For the most part, I expected to take pictures of the things I found, with the idea it would be proof enough to convince The Guard to unseal the main doors.

I wished for Mica's guidance here, for sure. Even before he was legally old enough to do so, he happily wielded a scuba tank. I got my certification this past winter as part of my preparation to join The Guard. As much as I loved being underwater, the whole scuba thing wasn't my idea of a good time; I found it claustrophobic and limiting. Blake kept insisting I use it tonight, in case the lab flooded when we opened the door.

But, I didn't listen to him. I knew I could handle it a lot better without scuba tanks than with them.

Even after I knocked down his scuba argument, he kept trying to talk me out of the whole thing. He cited honor, my place in The Guard, the rules, and a host of other excuses, that added up to him caring more about regulations than he cared about people. He was the epitome of his grandfather Stoney's progeny.

"We can get in there without you sneaking in," he pleaded. "We just need more time to convince them. We can ask our grandfathers again."

I didn't agree they could be convinced.

"Blake, how many days are you going to let go by before you realize they're hiding something important? We need to make our own solution."

We went back and forth for an hour, fighting on the driveway between our houses, voices and tempers escalating until Blake punched a tree and I walked to my house and locked the door. He hadn't bothered me since.

That thought was hardly comforting when I was packing up above ground, already feeling like I was drowning.

Helix was already in place by the lab when I snuck into the water by my house. My mom complicated the situation by coming home to have dinner with me. Feeling guilty for the extra time she'd been spending with Mica at the hospital, she tried to make up for it by making me eat. She brought both fried chicken and the news my dad finally found a flight back to civilization.

For seven days, he had supposedly been trying to get back. He was on a historic reenactment in an incredibly remote part of the Pacific, charting possible locations our ancestors had come from by captaining the same kind of boat. I say 'supposedly' because, even though I knew my dad loved Mica and me, I often felt he loved his work more. He lived for it. This dig was the culmination of ten years of writing papers and raising grant money, and was part of a lifelong passion project he'd finally gotten the University to support.

"So, he's pissed, right?" I asked mom, scarfing down a chicken leg as quickly as possible. Each bite stuck in my throat like I was swallowing bone and not meat. But, as soon as we finished eating, she headed back to the hospital, and I needed her out of the house, fast.

"Of course not, Cami."

"Come on, Mom; he gave up an entire summer on-Island for this. There's no way he's happy about coming home early."

"There's nothing more important to your father and me than you two. No matter how busy we get or how far away we are. You know that, right?"

I couldn't handle the earnest question, or look her in the eye and give her the confirmation she needed, and perhaps even deserved. It's not that my parents ever did us any harm, but they definitely subscribed to the 'It takes a village' parenting philosophy that was common on Pinhold.

Because of that, I'd spent equal number of hours with many of the other adults on-Island. My dad was always traveling or researching, and my mom was a study in extremes. When we were younger, we were sheltered and monitored as much as possible, until Doc asked her to supervise the hospital. Since then, she's spent all her time building the hospital and running the show. It seemed to have replaced her obsession with us.

As always, I wished for a little more balance from my relationship with my mom, especially because my dad was no better. When he was on a project, or teaching, his work consumed him. Summers off put him in the house or at work for The Guard, where he was way too much in our business. We were allowed to go around town, primarily because he was all over the place.

Mica had been the most constant presence in my life, with Blake and Shay coming in a close second and third.

"Then make the hospital do more for him," I pleaded.

"Cami, you have to believe we are—all of us—doing everything we can to help your brother. I understand you feel we were slow to act when it was just Shay, but that's never been true. We're exploring every single option at top speed."

As our potential heart-to-heart quickly morphed into a press conference, I called her on the administrator-speak.

"How much do you know about the fertility treatments you had for us, Mom?"

"Why would you ask me that?" She looked perplexed.

"Just curious," I said. "With all the time we're spending in the hospital, I'm just curious how it worked."

"Well, I'm happy to give you some literature from the hospital that details the process," she said.

"Okay, thanks," I said slowly. "But, wasn't it sort of different for you?"

"Well, the solution was in its infancy. Doc pioneered the process we needed here on-Island, because of our unique environmental factors."

"How did you decide the fertility treatments were necessary?"

"We were losing babies, Cami. We'd tried everything else. We were desperate," she said, wiping a tear from her cheek.

"Aren't you losing babies now?" I asked. It was a sucker punch, but I had to give it one last-ditch effort. I truly didn't think my mom was seeing the parallel.

"We have thrown everything we can think of at this," my mother said. Her voice became the scary whisper she'd perfected when Mica and I were very young and she needed to talk and tamp down her anger simultaneously.

"So, maybe you need to think of new things?" I asked, rhetorically.

"Don't even start in on Doc again. He's working on this around the clock, and has talked to many experts. None of them know more than he does; none of them could help."

With that, her barely-contained sobs broke out, and I found myself as dumbfounded by her tears as Helix and Blake had been on the pier when I'd cried. I wondered if my mom's tears were as orchestrated as mine had been then. Even if I didn't believe all her words, I recognized the pain in her eyes. It matched my own. I knew this was even harder on her than it was on me, if that was possible. I put my hand on her shoulder and leaned in to give her a hug. She gripped me tightly and sobbed into my hair, which made me want to cry, too.

But I couldn't afford the time to don the weepy sister hat and join my mom's sobs. I needed to put on my warrior helmet.

Any chance I had for real answers were drowned in her tears. Using this time to further figure out if she knew what the Doc was hiding, or if she was just as in the dark as the rest of us, was no longer possible. Since we weren't getting to the bottom of anything new, I needed more than anything else to just get her out the door.

"I know you're doing everything you can, Mom, really," I said, choking on the words just like the chicken. Assuaging her guilt was making it hard for me to breathe. But, it worked.

Fifteen minutes later, she was on her way back to the hospital, and I was closing up my waterproof gear and attaching my iPhone to my arm. Confirming Helix was in place was the last step.

fifteen

WE DECIDED ON sunset as the best time for the mission. The waning light made it hard to see anything on the water's surface, even more so than when it was fully dark at night. In addition to the quality of the fading sun's glow, it was also our own private Pinhold Changing of The Guard.

At shift switch, the people who'd been on all day went back to the guardhouse with all the equipment. They spent twenty minutes with the night staff, while they exchanged information and discussed the conditions for the day. Then the night Guard went on duty.

Helix told me I would have, maybe, twenty-five minutes in the lab with the alarm down, but I needed to be in and out in twenty. The goal was to be already swimming away when the meeting was over and The Guard came back on duty.

The one thing I knew I could count on The Guard for, was a prompt adherence to schedule. With military precision, the schedule had changed little over the past fifty years. I was counting on that now.

Although I felt like I was advertising my interest in the old lab, I'd discussed it with very few people in town. Between the talk there was and the alarm going off the other night, I'd been concerned the Lighthouse was going to be under more watch than usual. Luckily, that only seemed to be the case for a couple of days after the alarm incident. Things seemed back to normal.

I called my dolphin and texted Helix at the same time, giggling to myself at the absurdity. Both actions accomplished the same thing in totally different ways. My dolphin seemed to respond to a series of three whistles, one long click, and one short one—it sounded a little like yodeling to me. Without fail, she always came over to me when she heard me make the call.

A minute after making the sound, I saw a picture of her swimming toward me in my head. Helix texted he was in place and no one else was around. I told him the dolphin was headed my way, too.

Everything was in place.

My heart pounded so fast I saw my chest pulsing under the skin of my wetsuit. I took a few deep breaths to calm myself and jumped off the dock, trying to diminish the splash as much as possible, just in case anyone was around.

The Guard said swimming alone on the beaches was against the rules. I wasn't swimming on the beach, but despite the semantics, The Guard wouldn't be supportive of my actions. I hoped the outcome would prove it was right.

Despite my nerves, I couldn't help but smile when my dolphin came up. It was a thrill to know I had gotten her sound on the first try.

It took me most of the summer to understand the repeated sounds identified her, and another two weeks to be able to produce the noises properly. Since getting this sound down, she came right away and I somehow knew when she was en route.

I pulled my pack onto my back, and checked in with Helix when my phone was submerged. It appeared to work, so we set off.

Swimming together had become second nature for me. I kept up with her speed, breathed and went under as she did. The setting sun broke on the waves, tossing prisms of pink light above and below the water line. My gray eyes processed all the information so quickly; I never needed to squint.

We flew over and under the water, and around to the other side of the Island. The water was almost completely shadowed by the time we got to the jetty closest to the Lighthouse.

Per my plan with Helix, this was where we were supposed to stop. He would turn the alarm off. I looked to the beach and saw him—a speck off to the side of the Lighthouse. He had his headphones in, head tilted back, looking deceptively like any other beach bum watching the sun go down. It likely wouldn't be obvious to anyone else on the beach that he was using his iPhone to interrupt the alarm signal in the lighthouse.

He'd promised an interruption in service, based on the system tests that were frequently conducted between the alarm company and The Guard. The twenty-minute window of downtime wouldn't trigger a warning if it were turned off on the inside. Whatever software Helix had cooked up, was supposed to ensure it did.

With my fingers and toes crossed, I texted him to go. The six seconds between my message and his return were the longest of my life. Eventually, his text came back, "*Go now.*"

With one look at my dolphin, we did. Staying in her shadow, under her flank, I swam the entire five hundred foot distance underwater. We arrived at the door, and I, very quietly and carefully, surfaced to take in as much air I could handle. I'd been testing myself by the dock all week; I could stay underwater for up to four minutes without coming up for air. If I stayed under for eight minutes— which I could do—I would exhaust myself so horribly I wouldn't be able to do anything else.

I hoped that four minutes would be enough time to get me in the door and into the inner lab. One look through the window confirmed the alarm light was off. It also seemed there was air in the lab because it looked dry. I hoped it would stay that way after I opened the door. When we went down the week earlier to scout the location, my dolphin aimed her sonar at the lock and cracked it open. We left it hanging on the door so I could come back.

With a quick prayer to my dolphin, Mica, and every god I could think of, I dove and pulled the ancient lock off of the door. So far so good. Now, I had to jimmy open the outer door and get inside.

The gray metal was rusted in spots and hard to move. I put the heavy metal lock back through the outer part of its hole for leverage and pulled. The creak pounded in my ears—and clearly my dolphin's, as well- but the door barely moved.

My dolphin examined the door, turning her head slightly to gaze at it with her right eye.

When she shifted to face front, I knew she was about to blast the door. Before I had a chance to stop her, she did. Her sonic waves pushed the door sideways on the frame, leaving an open triangle that was too small for me to fit. No matter how I twisted and turned, I was unable to get more than my head and one arm through.

Only an arm's length away was a glass door. It looked like the kind on the deck at my house. It made sense the same person had provided all the doors in town, which hopefully meant the door locked the same as well. Ours had a lever you could pop from the outside if you knew where to find it.

That trick had saved me millions of times when I left home without my key; I prayed it would help me now, but I had to get to it first. I couldn't do that without more air.

As slowly and as quietly as possible, I snuck to the surface to breathe. The countdown clock on my phone read sixteen minutes left. I knew fifteen was my better goal.

My dolphin swam to the surface with me, breathing noisily through her blowhole. I shushed her, realizing after I did it was a pointless action about a noise she couldn't control. I spent an extra second glancing around for people or boats near enough to see us. Finding none, I went back underwater to take another stab at the door.

Using my feet for leverage, I used my hands to push within the triangle the dolphin had made. In the ton of effort expended, I only managed to move the door an inch. My dolphin watched and lined herself up, ready to blast again.

I held up my hands, wanting her to stop and hoping she would somehow understand, worried a second blast would fracture the glass door beyond the metal, and flood the lab. One last time, I lined up, feet and hands ready to push and pull again.

With all the pressure in my legs, I pushed at the door. It flew open and pushed me back, knocking me out of the way. It started to swing closed again, so I pushed past my dolphin, determined to get through. I was inches away, when a hand flew out from the door and kept it from sealing shut.

And even though I was underwater, where no one could hear, I screamed.

Blake went to work while I recovered, opening the interior door and dragging me in. I gasped in the stale air as he slid the door closed behind us, pushing it a little harder than I was comfortable with, considering its age and importance.

"Easy, Blake. If you break it, we can't get out."

"Right—or it'll crack and flood us in. But this never concerned you before, Cami, so why worry about it now?"

"What are you doing here?" I said, coughing; a sulfur taste in the stale air.

"Let's try 'thank you?'" he asked, whacking me on the back to help me catch my breath. "You wouldn't have gotten in here if it wasn't for me."

"I was doing fine. You got in the way—so stay out of it now. Be a good little soldier and keep watch or something. I have things to do."

"Excuse me for trying to make sure you don't die. I don't have high hopes for a place that has the same sliding glass door as my grandparents' patio for protection."

I took a deep breath. I didn't have time to argue; I had to focus. Distractions of any kind—even ones with the misplaced-hero concept—weren't something I could afford. I rolled my eyes and put my bag on an empty table, taking out my camera so I could get to work.

I sent Helix a quick text to let him know I was in. I had ten minutes. From what I could tell at first glance, there were three key areas that needed investigating.

The lab didn't look so different from the new ones at the hospital or in the research center. I was grateful for the little bits of time I'd spent in both this summer, because I had an idea of where I needed to look. Ignoring Blake, I approached a row of large metal cylinders plugged in against a wall.

A quiet hum and soft green lights told me they were on, despite the rust and mold that stained the silver. It smelled damp, and I looked around for leaks. In the corner, above a bank of file cabinets, a wet stream was actively running down a crumbling plaster wall. It had clearly seen its fair share of water damage.

Drips coming through the ceiling in the middle of the room were less of a concern, because they were likely from the heating and air conditioning unit servicing the main part of the lighthouse. But the file cabinets needed handling—that wall didn't look like it was likely to hold.

"Make yourself useful," I said, tossing the plastic file folder pack to Blake. "Take anything that looks important. Whatever will fit."

He rolled his eyes at me, about to argue, but I turned my back before he could say anything. It took every ounce of willpower I had to keep my eyes tuned to the task at hand, but I did it. A slight glance in the rusted silver showed a reflection of him prying the cabinet open, getting to work.

The humming of the third cylinder caught my attention, even though it wasn't first in the line. It sounded louder than the others. Closer inspection showed some green goo leaking around the seal. I snapped a couple shots on my iPhone and texted Helix. In case I didn't make it back, he would know there was something in here worth looking at after all.

There were five cylinders in all. Besides number three, they looked untouched. Each stood as tall as my waist, and had no less than five tubes going in and out, connecting to one another. I'd seen equipment like this before in the hospital; it was used for testing and experiments, but that's about all I knew. I documented the serial number on each tank and tried to find a brand name or other identifying information.

There was a plaque at the bottom of the first one, but the letters had been ruined with damp and rust. I zoomed in and captured as much detail as possible, hoping it would be recognizable to someone—even if it wasn't recognizable to me.

A noise outside the window to the sea caught my attention. My dolphin was looking in the window, which I found encouraging. I walked towards the glass, hoping it wasn't a warning someone was around. My watch showed we had eight minutes left, and there were other things I needed to accomplish.

The dolphin shook her head at me, her perma-grin offering comfort as it always had. I knew it was structural and not emotional, her smile never failed to bring about the same response in me. The panic I'd felt when I thought she was sending a warning disappeared, replaced with quiet confidence.

She was so secure in every movement, action, and interaction. Guided by instinct, there seemed to be no room in her psyche for doubt or delay. I took my strength from her and looked around the room, taking in details I'd failed to notice on my first glance around.

Old posters lined one wall: faded, but visible depictions of human and dolphin anatomy, as well as the in-utero development timeline for both species. I looked closer—the dolphin development images were something I hadn't come across before. Up until month six, the dolphin and human fetuses looked remarkably similar.

Clearly, I wasn't the first to notice. Closer inspection revealed notes written on both posters—difficult to decipher, but there nonetheless. I pulled each poster off the wall, folding them inside one another. There wasn't time to do things twice so I immediately took them over to the paper pack Blake was working to fill.

I carefully folded the posters one more time to fit, praying the folds and the age of the paper wouldn't render the handwriting illegible. I took quick note of the other papers that were already inside: charts, diagrams, and textbook stuff. My heart sank; I saw nothing proprietary or obviously written by Doc.

"This is a waste of time, Cami," Blake said, slamming a drawer shut before opening the fourth cabinet on the wall. The drawer popped into place, shaking the entire bank of metal and tilting the end unit so that it banged into the banking wall. A loud crack preceded a dust blast as bits of old plaster came loose and landed at my feet.

Blake's result-oriented anger bugged me, causing my thoughts to flash to Kaleb. He'd love it in here: mysterious and illegal was right up his alley. I couldn't help but wish he was the one here with me; his passion for the process might yield information neither Blake nor I were able to see.

Despite the lack of relevant files, I refused to be discouraged.

"Keep looking," I instructed, and turned back to the science experiments, blocking both boys from my head. We were well into the single digits on the time we had left. I figured I had time to find one more thing before we needed to bolt.

A last look around confirmed the file cabinets and the canisters were the points of interest, so I headed back over to see if I could garner any additional detail on what was cooking in the containers. They had remained on, and locked down in the same place, since the lab had been sealed off so many years ago, but there wasn't a clear reason why. From the outside, it appeared they were empty.

While it was important to note they were here, I feared it wasn't important enough to justify my break-in or to get The Guard to unseal the door properly and take a deeper look.

Running my hands around the top of the third container, I looked for a lever or a latch—something that would let me raise the hatch to check out what was inside. The other containers were too tightly sealed, but the little leak at the bottom of this one indicated a breach of some kind.

Hopefully, it hadn't ruined whatever was inside, because in that moment I decided if I could get it open and get it out, I was taking whatever was in there with me when we left. I closed my eyes, reached around the back, searching the seam for a release. I felt it then: a lip with a hinge. This was where the lid came up, but that didn't get me any closer to in.

Moving both hands to the back, I inched my fingertips around both sides of the circle, looking for any break in the symmetry. I found a bump on the right side, and pressed it in. Nothing happened. I tried to remember the centrifuges in the lab; I'd decided these were the same thing. They had magnet releases that were coded to the cards of the scientists who had clearance to unlock each specific one.

These were older than those, so there was hope they were easier to open, but time wasn't on my side.

"Cami!" Blake yelled, appearing suddenly in front of my face. My eyes flashed open, startled right out of my trance. Pulled in by his intensity, I paused and briefly forgot what it was I was trying to do.

"Cami! We have to go!" Blake yelled, grabbing my shoulders.

I glanced at my watch. We had two minutes left. I caught my breath, intending to use every last second to get the container open, or disconnected from the wall.

"I need to get this open. Can you stop yelling at me and try to help?"

"Cami, look!" With a force made stronger with fear, he turned me physically to face the entrance, which was also the only exit we had.

The simple glass door, that had done its job successfully for years, began to crack. Spider veins on the surface were visible, even from where I stood twenty feet away. There was water rising outside, too, no doubt getting in from the small triangle my dolphin had blasted through the exterior door.

The one-hundred-and-twenty seconds I'd been counting on were disappearing quickly. I sucked in the stale air and turned my attention back to the equipment.

"If the lab floods, the experiments will be buried. We have to get these out."

"If the lab floods, we could be trapped. Best case, caught. Worst case, dead! Disaster case: we die and everything gets ruined. Leave it, Cami. We have to go."

Blake's warnings got a signal boost by similar squawking from my dolphin outside, chatter that while harder to decipher was more difficult for me to ignore. I felt her fear in every fiber of my body, in the very center of my brain where Mica used to talk. It was very real danger she was reporting; but, for my twin's sake, I needed at least one more minute to try again.

"If we die down here, it doesn't help Mica at all," Blake screamed.

But I obsessed. The irony of ignoring my own imminent death in an attempt to save my brother's life wasn't lost on me, but I didn't worry. The instincts that had led me this far, also told me this wasn't the time to give up.

The pressure of the water wall, the dolphin's voice, and Blake's ripe fear all faded as time expanded in my brain. I shook off his hold and reached for Mica's fishing spear that was hooked on the back of my belt. Raising it above my head, I brought it down on the glass case.

The crack was loud, but ineffective. Small lines appeared, similar to the ones in the glass door up front, which were multiplying every second. I tried again and the top on the machine stood guard, protecting its mystery like a dragon guarding her treasure.

Suddenly, Blake grabbed the spear from my hand and held it above his head, striking down on the metal. His brute strength did further damage, but it wasn't enough.

My phone buzzed, reminding us the real world waited, even if the ocean that pushed against the door didn't . The clicking outside the window caught my attention. My dolphin's smile was no longer there; she was frightened and confused. I felt invisible waves pulsing on my body— as if she was reading me to see why I didn't understand the problem.

I brought her attention to the metal   along the wall, where Blake prepared to smash it again. I pushed him out of the way, landing on top of him right before the blast shook the equipment and disconnected the fifth canister from the wall. The hook Blake held dug painfully into my side and I felt relief as I jumped off him and went to grab the centrifuge. I didn't realize it had dug into him even worse.

"Let me get it, Cami! Just grab the bag and go!" he yelled.

Five seconds of struggle felt like forever as Blake yanked the wires from the wall and disconnected number five. I had the bag on my back, and the door opened right in time. I barely remembered to remind us both to breathe.

We headed for the surface after slamming the doors shut. I prayed they would hold so Helix could re-engage the alarm, and buy us time to get away. Faint blue lights below us in the water told me he had done it. That part had worked, but we had to swim fast to get away.

I hadn't planned on Blake or the large piece of equipment he carried. As winded as we were, weighted with extra cargo, swimming against the current underwater was almost impossible. Blake began to lag behind, forcing me to surface in order to figure out what was going on. Struggling to breathe and favoring his left side, Blake whispered for me to leave him and let him swim behind.

"Not happening," I told him, taking the canister from him. We went on like this for a while. My dolphin occasionally nudged him from behind.

He slowed even further, and I glanced at my dolphin, begging silently for help. It was dark, but the moon was high. We'd rounded the bend on the side of the Island, finally swimming out of the shadows and into a little bit of light.

Struggling, I pulled Blake along the waves, swimming against the current, heading for home. He was heavy in the water and getting heavier. At first, he kicked and paddled, but he had stopped moving and was fading fast.

Pausing long enough to catch my breath, I took a good look at him. Despite the summer water temps and his wetsuit, he began to shiver. In order to save him, I was going to have to let the centrifuge drown.

Sadly, I let it go. Then, I started trying to figure out how to get a hold on Blake. Reaching around his torso in an effort to get a better grip, took me three tries. The broad chest that I loved so much, made it challenging.

I felt a tug on my belt and saw the diving hook had come unfurled, adding to our drag in the water. One-handed, I struggled to pull it up. My dolphin broke the surface with the hook held in her mouth.

I panicked because one of the pointed ends was covered in slime and blood. I was ready to cry, thinking it was hers. Instead, she put the hook gently in my hand and opened her mouth, showing me she was free from injury.

The tears I'd held back since our terrifying exit erupted from my eyes like a volcano, as an image of Blake injured appeared in my head. I looked down to find him passed out completely. I turned his shoulder gently and found a rip in his wetsuit, a matching one in his skin. The hook had gone in his shoulder when I'd fallen on him in the lab and, in order to save us both, he yanked it out without saying a thing.

My dolphin tucked her head under and gently put her rostrum on the injury, drawing a faint groan from Blake. Good news; he wasn't out cold.

She backed away slowly, as to not disturb the water, and aimed her snout right at him. Flashing back to the first night I met her, I was reminded of how she aimed her energy at me and stopped my blood. With all I'd learned since then, I knew it had something to do with her bio-sonar, but, beyond that, I had no clue. I prayed she could do it again and it would work for Blake.

Backing away another foot, she looked out her right eye, turned her melon toward us and let out a blast. I felt a pulse of light as well; her energy penetrating both of us.

Unfortunately, the extent of his injury appeared to be much worse than mine had been. She tried three more blasts, nearly stopping the flow. But, she paused, looked at me, and shook her head.

He couldn't handle another blast. I understood imm-ediately; my molecules felt like they'd been scrambled, too.

I nodded and adjusted my hold. At this point, I was getting cold. Getting Blake more help couldn't wait.

I adjusted my body to swim backwards, with Blake on top, in the traditional lifeguard rescue hold, and began to move. I needed to go quickly and carefully; no simple feat, given his weight, the current, and my own level of exhaustion, when help came from below.

Blake's dolphin came up on our side, stopping under his good arm. I considered the offer and imagined the mechanics. Had his shoulder not been injured, the dolphin could have supported him on one side with me on the other. But given his physical condition, it wasn't going to work. In my mind's eye, I pictured him lying across the dolphin's back, but the tapered shape didn't leave enough room behind the dorsal fin. Pulling Blake along the animal's side, I attempted to get him up and onto the slippery gray surface, but I couldn't lift him high enough without help.

My dolphin breached the surface and came to Blake, too. Staying next to the other dolphin and just under Blake's body, I turned him diagonally and swam on her back. The dolphins made their way together, slowly, toward our dock while I held on to Blake for dear life—his life. Despite our recent battles, my life was worth very little to me with him gone, too.

I called Billy as soon as we got to the dock. Luckily, he was home. The Medicopter took him straight to the hospital for a CAT scan—our hospital had now approved them as a first-line protocol in these situations. He was in a coma, similar to Mica's and Shay's, but he also had an obvious injury, so his situation was potentially more dangerous.

Stoney rushed in, asking questions about why we'd been in the water at night. I didn't have an answer, but Helix talked about some experiment for school we were helping with.

They had no reason not to believe it, thanks to Helix. The alarms went back online and no one was saying a word about the guardhouse or the lab. So far it seemed no one knew what we had done.

I went to Mica's room at the hospital, to hold his hand. I confessed my sins to his lifeless form until my mom found me and ordered me home. Knowing I needed to stash all the equipment from our ill-fated mission, for once I didn't argue.

The sun refused to shine the next morning, as reluctant to face the day as I was, now Blake was hurt. The sticky gray fog matched my mood. Clouds of new information were stuck in loops running through my brain.

I stayed up all night going through files from the lab. It took me hours to find anything new. But I did: Clinical Protocol—Clearance Level, Five.

The protocols detailed in this report were different from any I saw before. This went beyond simply helping to support conception, and into the creepy space of eugenics. Using brand-new technology, Doc isolated a specific strand of DNA, cloned it, and wove it into every single one of the ten of us born my year. There were records of many failed experiments until he perfected the sequence. It seemed the added combination of the extra DNA strand made the cells grow with immunity to the threats that had been causing our problems. All the other protocols had been to help the moms carry the enhanced babies to term.

I called Billy to check on Blake.

"He doesn't have the ear damage," Billy said, kindly spending time on the phone with me, which was way more than I had expected, given the early hour and my part in the whole mess. "We're hoping his coma isn't like the rest. He had a bad concussion and lost a ton of blood. "Now, you need to tell me how this really happened, Cami. I'm not buying the story you told Stoney. Tell me everything you can think of that might help."

I took a gulp of air, swore him to secrecy, and caught him up with everything I had learned. I finished with, "It goes beyond the ears and eyes. It relates to our DNA. Doc messed with it and made a few different recessive genes prominent so we'd have the best chance of helping the Island population recover. It went silent on his end of the phone. The sky was yellowing a bit; I prayed for some illumination of my own. "I hoped you would understand it, Billy," I said, hoping to nudge him along. "What about the brain thing? Do other people's brains look like mine, and Mica's, and Blake's?"

"There are differences in the size, but it's impossible to tell what else might be different. Half of Darwen's, Mica's, and Shay's brains just appear to be shut down. So, maybe this is why," he said, with a huge sigh. "I want to see the files myself—to make sure I understand the same things from the notes as you. I still need to know how Blake got hurt."

"Trying to get the proof from the experiments out of the old lab," I said, thinking sadly of the canister that was somewhere under twelve feet of liquid blue. "There were centrifuges—like in the lab where Celeste works. I think they had experiments in them. We were trying to get them off the wall to bring to you."

"And that's when Blake got hurt?"

"Yep. A dive hook. I didn't see it happen. We both fell down, and I think it went into his arm. He didn't say anything right away, because we were in a serious hurry. I honestly didn't even know he was hurt," I said, feeling remorse for paying so much more attention to the equipment than Blake.

"So, he was okay at first?"

"Yes. We left the lab and swam almost halfway. And then, he just kind of stopped and couldn't go on. He passed out when I hauled him back to you."

"I'm impressed. That's not easy to do."

"I had a little help."

"What?" he said, finally sounding angry with me. Which I felt I deserved. "Who saw you?"

"Don't worry," I said. "They won't talk." How was I going to explain this one?

"How do you know? Breaking and entering is serious— it was Island property—Guard property, no less. . . ."

"Billy, calm down. No one human saw us. A couple of dolphins helped carry us back."

"You are incredibly lucky they found you," he said, awe in his tone.

"One of them was with us at the lab—the whole time, really."

"I . . . I . . .I. Wow," Billy said, at a loss for words for the first time I could ever remember.

I hung up with Billy and was greeted, almost instantly, with another hello. This one was from my dolphin and I was so grateful to see her. With everything we had been through together, I felt closer to her at the moment than anyone else.

She looked at me, looked next door, and looked back at me. A picture of Blake appeared in my head. She was asking how he was. I considered how similar the image was to those I shared with Mica. A picture of Mica flitted into my brain, and she nodded emphatically over and over again.

"Really?" I said, out loud, shaking my head at her. "Are you trying to tell me you know how to—talk? Like he and I do?"

She nodded, and I smiled, feeling for the first time in forever I wasn't so alone.

Laughter behind my back distracted me from my conversation with my water friend, sounding so much like Blake, it made my head spin. My body followed, hoping for a miracle. In spite of the similarity of sound, the person behind me was as different from Blake as an identical twin could be.

Kaleb's arrival shook me and sent me into panic mode, because I didn't know what to do. The dolphin immediately caught on to my stress and started breaching and blowing air, coming up way too close to the dock for her own safety and flashing concerned images of a light, colorful Blake and dark Kaleb in my mind. I saw them both from her perspective—Kaleb looked like a black-and-white photo come to life.

His hair was longer than Blake's and colored jet black with hints of blue. I almost expected him to wear guy-liner, but he didn't. His eyes looked identical to his brother's, but they didn't feel the same to me.

I forced my gaze from his chest, where the outline of the piercing he'd done online showed through his summer shirt. He definitely looked scarier than Blake, but I knew he wasn't. Seeing him brought up those old feelings of abandonment and anger because he got kicked out and left me here. But he was back now. And for that he deserved a little gratitude and a proper explanation to my dolphin friend.

"It's okay," I said, jumping in the water in my shorts and tee to swim her way and pat her head. "He's Blake's brother. He's not going to hurt us. Or Blake," I said to the dolphin. Yes, I'd started talking to her. It was comforting and she seemed to understand. "No, he won't hurt me either. He's here to help, I think."

"You are here to help, I hope?" I said to him, when my dolphin was calm enough I could turn back toward Kaleb.

"We all know I wouldn't be invited back on-Island if it weren't to help golden-boy Blake."

I looked at Kaleb, keeping my mouth shut. I had nothing nice to say, but I felt somepity. Being that unwelcoming couldn't feel good.

"Save it for him, Cami. I don't need your sympathy," he said, pushing his hair away from his eyes, then shaking it right back where it had been. I thought of Blake moving his hand from front to back in his own hair. Their opposition was evident everywhere, in big picture details, and tiny habits as well.

"I'm glad to see you're talking to the dolphins again. That's something I didn't expect."

I looked at him, rolling my eyes. Kaleb always loved to speak in riddles, and right now I didn't have the time.

"C'mon, I'm here, and I saved the day. Don't I get, like, Guard points or something for that?"

"What exactly did you do?" I asked, softening a bit. His sarcasm should have offended me. Instead, it made me feel like a little kid, bringing me back to days when the most serious injury any of us had, was a scraped knee.

"I gave him my very own blood," he said. "What could be more heroic than that?"

"Didn't have a choice, did you?" I asked, unwilling to cut him quite so much slack.

"Nah, they'd been ordering me back since Mica went down. Sorry about that, by the way."

I shrugged, struggling to hold in the tears. My dolphin started clucking at me again, and an image of the canister appeared in my head.

"So, what's the deal with this canister thing?" he asked, and I looked back at him with a gasp.

"What did Billy tell you?"

"Billy barely talked to me; just took my blood like the mindless Guard vampire he is, and told me to go wait by myself back here."

"Poor Kaleb. You must really like being the black sheep."

"Yeah, fine. But, your friend here seems to know where this thing you're looking for is. So, do we follow her?"

I spent all of ten seconds wondering how Kaleb knew what was happening, and then I moved. I unhooked the kayak and dropped it in the water, ordering him in.

"Sorry about this," I said to my dolphin, "but I don't know if he remembers how to swim."

Kaleb just laughed at me as I maneuvered us away from the dock.

We followed my dolphin in silence, coming up to the old jetty where I thought Blake had lost consciousness. I jumped in.

"Stay put," I said to Kaleb and dove down under the kayak. The container sat twenty feet from the surface on the ocean floor, broken into tiny bits.

LATER—MUCH LATER—I asked Kaleb how he knew what the dolphin was talking about, or that she was talking at all.

"We used to talk to them when we were little, Cami," he said, sounding disappointed. "It was you who decided not to listen anymore."

"When we were, like, five. It was pretend," I sputtered, sounding like the 5-year-old I had once been.

When we were really young, the dolphins came around daily, begging for food on the docks. Back then, we'd given it to them, but eventually laws prohibited anyone from feeding them. After that, we had a few years of tough love. The adults on-Island were strict with us and the dolphins. So, the dolphins stopped coming and relearned how to get fish on their own.

"For the record, I never thought it was pretend. It's one of the things I miss most about this place," he said, shooting a look my way.

His thoughts were so sad. A rush of memories came back, and I gasped when I realized I was actually seeing inside his head. His thoughts included symbols and pictures that were close to the ones I'd gotten from the dolphin.

When I looked at him in shock, he confirmed they were real.

"Can everyone else do this, too?" I asked.

"No, we're special. Don't you know that?" he sneered. More images came into my head; and I felt his anger growing. Minutes into the conversation, I realized how much information I was getting from the images in his brain.

It was a connection that, before today, I'd only ever shared with Mica. My mind instantly went to Blake, because somehow it felt like I was cheating on him. Sharing the equivalent of a twin link with Kaleb made me feel bad—as if I was leaving both our twin brothers behind.

Kaleb and I stayed together for a few more hours talking, as I ran through the whole summer with him. I needed to speak to someone, and the sad truth of the matter was that he was literally the only one available.

"Go back again and tell me exactly what the dolphin did to you?" he asked. His interest and ability to listen was oddly comforting and impressive. His completely fresh perspective was really helpful. And, he saw most of what Blake knew, too.

As I went through the story with him again, I saw in his thoughts exactly what we needed to do.

"You need to get Mica in the water with his dolphin," Kaleb said. And I agreed.

Kaleb had been back in town for only a number of hours and already I was questioning my sanity. He had me believing my conversations with my dolphin were more than imaginary and in fact, a point of historical and genealogical importance. He also had me believing I could hear his thoughts in my head, which was especially disturbing because, even though they were filtered through a crazy-colored Kaleb window, it meant I could see Blake's thoughts, too.

In one specific way, it seemed Kaleb and Blake agreed. Blake had been constantly on my case to go to The Guard with everything we knew. He wanted to be straight with Stoney. Kaleb thought we should handle getting Mica into the water on the up and up, too.

He even had me convinced, that the best way to go about this was to convince my parents to help, which was the craziest part of it all. Breaking and entering an abandoned lab was one thing. Getting Mica out of the hospital and into the water was something I couldn't do on my own.

sixteen

MY DAD DIDN'T even make it in the door before I was wrapping my arms around him and drenching his shirt with my tears.

"You've done good Cami. Stronger than I could have ever hoped," he said, tugging on my ponytail before giving me a big hug. His brown eyes peered into my silver ones, and it felt good, like being truly seen. My tears spilled as he squeezed me, tight. I didn't even mind that I couldn't breathe.

"I know this hasn't been easy on you," he said. "But, I have a surprise. A good one, I think." I tried to smile when he gave me a sympathetic look and wiped away a tear. "Mica's coming home tonight," he said calmly.

My eyes sprang open, tears drying immediately as my brain shifted, jumping in a million directions all at once.

"It's just for the night," he said, filling me in, even though I hadn't asked the question. "But since he's not in any immediate danger, I really, really want us to sleep under the same roof."

I nodded, overwhelmed. If I needed a sign from the universe Kaleb's plan was worth a shot, then this, for sure, was it.

Getting Mica into the water from home would be a thousand times easier than getting him into the water from the hospital. For the first time in a while, it seemed I was getting a lucky break; although Kaleb coming home had been a lucky break, too. After my conversation with my dad, I got in the water to go find my dolphin.

Despite my exhaustion, I was desperate to go for a swim. I had so much to figure out before Mica came home tonight. Being with her energized me, like I was in the zone of the best race without getting physically exhausted. It felt like a whole different part of my brain took over, while the part I used on land got a much-needed break.

I found her offshore taking a nap. She was so still she barely moved. For a minute, I stayed quiet, taking the time to watch her.

My mom said she used to watch us sleeping when Mica and I were babies; I never understood why. She said it was the only time we were still enough for her to really see us. There was magic in the stillness. As my dolphin slept, I understood, finally, what my mother meant.

My dolphin was so beautiful—stunning and shining in the sun, surrounded by a faintly glowing pinkish light. Incredibly, she slept with one eye open, bobbing over and under the surface. When she woke, I realized exactly what was happening.

There was no gradual awareness, no natural snooze alarm. Instead, it was simply like she had half the lights off in a room, and a quick switch turned them all back on again. I prayed that once I got Mica in the water, Mica's brain would do that, too.

As we swam, she showed me pictures. Because Kaleb opened me up to the possibility, I paid attention and understood them all. Once she realized I was getting it, she started flooding my brain with impressions, feelings, and memories.

She shared with me the true history of the dolphin twins. It wasn't just about her and her brother, or me and mine, or my "clique" of five sets of twins. Throughout the history on Pinhold, dolphins and people shared a real connection that went beyond legends.

They swam together and communicated freely as part of daily life. Her memories of my people and her pod were linked together. All of our rites and rituals—the weekly drum circle, the Surf Carnival—were truly part of her world.

She showed me the dark times, when they had to travel far away after the oil spill, when it took them so long to find their way home and then they had to leave again because of all the fishing boats. Some of these memories, weren't hers. They were images that had been passed down through multiple generations and on to her—including ones about the times leading up to her birth.

Like Gramps telling me how bad it had been before the fertility trials began, she knew of her pod's circumstances, too. It was her mother who led their pod back to the waters and came straight to the Doc, letting him do whatever it took to get her pregnancy to carry through. From the notes I had seen, it was obvious the tissues and blood samples he'd used in the DNA splicing, came from a dolphin. Now,

I knew that was her mother's DNA. My dolphin and I weren't just friends; we were part of the same gene pool.

When I showed her what I was thinking, she showed me it was nothing new. Everyone who talked to the dolphins and swam like them; shared DNA with them. Because our ancestors had, for the most part, stayed on-Island, we kept these traits, and they strengthened over years.

When babies stopped coming, and everyone started hopping to the Mainland, coupling up with new blood, the Elders panicked. Each generation had fewer and fewer people who had a dolphin twin, because so many of dolphins had left. They were worried that without drastic intervention they would lose it completely. That's when they gave Doc carte blanche to do whatever he needed to do. It obviously worked, as proven by the dominance in my generation of these typical Pinhold traits.

She showed me a combination of all the things I'd considered this summer. I saw how they were all interconnected, and all true. The military sonar did damage to the eardrum, causing our brains to short out.

In that case, the dolphin side of our brains took over. Mica, Shay, Darwen, and hopefully, Blake, were simply sleeping the dolphin way. The problem was the human side of their brains didn't know how to wake them up. If we could get them in the water with the dolphins, the dolphins could do it for them. We swam over to the bay docks where the dolphin tours left from, and found Gramps fixing one of the canoes. I hoped he could help me understand all of this.

Gramps was impressed with the amount of information I learned from my dolphin. He had a dolphin twin, too, but his communication was much more limited because, they hadn't found each other until Gramps was much older and he hadn't been able to understand his dolphin as well as I could understand mine.

"What you have learned this summer is more than most ever do. For many, they need years in The Guard to learn all of what you know. I've never gleaned any memories from him," he said.

"Do you think it's because he doesn't know the stories? My dolphin seemed to say that they all share the memories."

"Maybe he can't communicate them, or maybe I didn't understand everything as well as you did. You have a gift, child," he said with a small smile. "Which, I always knew."

"Did you know about the DNA thing?" I asked.

"No, but even if we had somehow found out, it wouldn't have been anything I could understand. I barely get it now. I'm impressed that you do. I can tell you that your awareness was exactly what we prayed for. So many Mainland marriages made us fear the things most important to us were being watered down. We worried we could lose them for good."

"You all were miracle babies, in every way. We simply felt gratitude and didn't look too hard at the how's and why's. Now, it seems, we're paying for that mistake. I wish there was more I could do."

"Say you'll help me," I pleaded, throwing myself in his arms. "None of this matters, if we can't wake Mica up. I know—with every bone in my body—that the only way to do that, is to get him in the water."

Gramps nodded and promised to meet me at the house, in an hour.

The conversation we had with my father didn't go quite as well. Having Mica come home, briefly, was one thing. Putting him in the water was totally another.

"That would be irresponsible," he said, sending a pointed 'Dad look' my way. "Almost as reckless as what you did with Blake the other night."

My dad raised his right eyebrow in a sharp corner, something he only did when he was incredibly suspicious. He stared at me until I was practically sweating, nervously trying to figure out what he knew, and how much of the truth I wanted to share.

"It was an accident with Blake."

"Yes, I know. What I don't understand is why you were out swimming with wetsuits, and weights, and hooks in the first place."

"We were helping Helix," I said, shrinking a little as the eyebrow continued inching up. He was definitely not buying the story, and I couldn't depend on him to support the rogue mission in quite the same way my grandfather seemed to.

I wasn't going to give up, though—not after all I had learned. Just because my parents couldn't see the truth, didn't mean I couldn't. In fact, it was precisely because I could see it, that I knew getting Mica in the ocean was the only answer.

I watched Mica sleep all night. Out of the glare of the hospital lights, away from the blips and bleeps and interruptions, his sleep seemed peaceful; much like my dolphin's. I couldn't hear his thoughts, but I knew more than ever he was alive, and that what I was about to do was truly going to help him.

My nerves were already off the charts when I heard a loud pop outside the second-story window. Luckily, my fear of the unknown lasted only seconds. I saw Kaleb in my mind before I looked out the window.

I went downstairs to let him in, and my heart jumped again at the sight. I was unused to seeing him. Even though he had never truly been out of my thoughts, the pictures of him in my brain barely connected with the guy who stood before me now.

Sure, I'd seen him since he left, but those images didn't stick in my head like the ones of him from before he moved away. Even then, he was the darker half of a pair, but that darkness was mostly internal, visible on the outside only if you knew where and how to look. Crazy, two-colored eyes had always flashed black lightning, as opposed to Blake's gray glow. Covering the larger portion of Blake's right eye and Kaleb's left was a large island of aqua blue that shared the pupil with the silver.

Now, Kaleb's outside was obviously darker, what with the hair, and the piercings, and all, but his eyes looked peaceful.

"Why do you look so smug?" I asked, whispering and shushing him as we went upstairs.

"I've been here less than twenty-four hours, and I'm sneaking into your house in the middle of the night," he said, smiling.

I interrupted him, forcing my whisper so he would really hear me.

"I'm glad this is amusing to you, but I'm with Blake now."

"He thinks you've broken up with him, so I wouldn't be too sure about that," he said, flashing my brain with images of all kinds of intimate moments with Blake that involved loving and fighting.

"Ugh, Kaleb, stay out of my head. Blake's, too," I said, while hypocritically using our new mental link to remind him to skip the creaky seventh step.

I'd convinced my parents to sleep in their own room—instead of in Mica's—to try and enjoy their first night back together. But, even without jet lag, my dad was a notoriously light sleeper. We couldn't take any unnecessary risks.

"I can't help it," he shrugged. "When I'm further away, or he's busy, I can block it out. But right now it's sort of unavoidable. I guess because he's out cold."

"Wait a second," I said, pulling him into the bathroom between Mica's room and mine. If I understood him properly, this was extremely important.

"Are you saying you're still hearing him?"

"Yeah. So what?" He rolled his eyes, so that they reflected the moonlight outside the window and flashed crazier than ever. For a moment, I wondered if he was putting me on—messing with me.

"Even I wouldn't do that," he said, sad from the thoughts passing through my head. "Not right now."

"So, really—you can hear Blake right now?" I asked, one more time.

"Yes. It's not news, Cami. It's just particularly annoying because he's got all this bullshit about you and The Guard on some sort of feedback loop. Can we just do the Mica thing now? I thought we were on some sort of timeline." I nodded and opened the door to Mica's room, stopping to turn around at the threshold.

"It's just that I can't hear Mica right now, and Alysha's link with Shay is down, too."

"Lucky, freaking, you," Kaleb hissed. "Can we do this?"

I nodded and moved over to the top of Mica's platform bed, indicating he should take his feet. Kaleb hearing Blake right now had to be good news for Blake. The fact his brain was working differently from Mica's and Shay's was also meaningful in the grand scheme of things, but not something I could delve into further tonight.

We only had a couple hours until dawn, and if this didn't work, I needed time to get Mica dried off and back into bed before my parents woke up.

"Don't think like that," Kaleb said, frustrated at the tear that rolled down my face. "It's not going to help."

Taking Mica down to the water was harder than I imagined. When we got to the dock, I jumped in. Kaleb lowered Mica into my arms, and got in himself.

In that moment, the silver fins of a pod of dolphins appeared, breaking up darkness between sea and sky. From the chatter it sounded like there were more than fifty of them—so many that the loud sounds were enough to draw attention to the water. We simply couldn't get caught. Even though the dolphins were always here, there weren't usually so many of them, especially not in the middle of the night.

"Shh," I whispered, putting my finger to my lips when my dolphin swam my way. She turned to her side, watching me with that all-seeing right eye, so I did it again.

She imitated me, making the same sound through her blowhole, getting water all over Kaleb, Mica, and me.

I felt nervous, terrified, and completely on edge, so when Kaleb's dolphin doused me, I lost it completely. Giggles burst from my mouth. At first, it felt fully inappropriate, like busting up at school.

But then, my dolphin nuzzled Mica gently, and I realized the giggles were her gift. Even at the most serious of times, my dolphin managed to inject the moment with play. Had it been anyone else, I would have been totally pissed off.

But by this point in the summer, I had learned some lessons from her. One of the most important things she'd taught me was that joy and fun were important all the time—no matter how awful things seemed. The joy she brought me, would bring success to this mission. Suddenly, I knew that everything was going to turn out all right.

I'd spent so many days resisting the love and joy I'd found with Blake, sure that what happened to Mica was some sort of punishment or universal revenge. In fact, the opposite was true. What Blake and I had together made me stronger and opened me up to all the other crazy things I had discovered this summer. He was right when he wanted me to go surfing in the ocean and I'd insisted on staying inside to surf the Internet. It was joy and play that brought answers—in the dolphins' world and in our own.

Kaleb was useless at helping me get Mica out to where all the dolphins swam in wait. He was clearly athletic, and had no problem doing the swim, despite his initial misgivings about the water. But, he had zero ability to support another person in the water. It fit, that he could take care of himself this way, but not anyone else. This was just one more reminder of how different he was from Blake.

Dragging along my lifeless brother, wrong and right were no longer obvious. Technically, what Kaleb and I were doing was wrong—even dangerous. It was against my parents' wishes and all rational thought, to put a comatose victim, who'd nearly drowned, back in the ocean.

It seemed crazy to trust the dolphins with his life. But somehow, because I had faith it would work, this was so very right.

Two more dolphins left the pod, to meet us halfway. They swam over to Mica, and pushed Kaleb and me away. One of them was Blake's dolphin, but the other one was someone new. He was my dolphin's twin. I suddenly knew he was bonded to Mica, just as my dolphin was bonded to me.

A picture of Blake, draped across our dolphins after he hurt his arm, flashed behind my eyes. I struggled to keep my arms and legs moving through the water, even as my mind was officially blown. Concentrating—though not too hard because, that wasn't their way—I relaxed for the first time since we hit the water and released Mica to our dolphin friends.

Since he wasn't injured the way Blake had been, I spread him out between the two dolphins, who came from underneath. They were close together, not touching. Mica's arms rested right above their fins and I felt confident he would stay put when they raised their heads, and began to swim.

Blake's dolphin seemed to recognize Kaleb, at least according to Kaleb's thoughts, but they didn't seem to have the same bond. Because of that, I realized Kaleb had no ability to keep up with the dolphins for the swim. He'd never done it before, and this wasn't the time to begin.

"Listen," I started, "I need you to go back to the dock and wait for us."

"Cami," Kaleb said, "I can't leave you alone."

"I can't do this with you here. Please skip the misguided chivalry, and let me do what we came out here to do."

Kaleb left, and we took off. Mica stayed put on his finned chariot and, in seconds, we were in the middle of the pod. Mica's dolphin delivered him into my arms. Then, all together, they swam around us. They swam faster and faster until they churned the water into a huge whirlpool encircling Mica and me.

Blake's dolphin moved to the front of the circle, swimming with the others, leading the charge. Mica's dolphins and mine stayed in the middle, close to us. The ocean moved so fast. Instead of feeling like it was dangerous and could bring me down, I felt lifted, buoyed, and safe. We were wrapped in a sacred swirl created by something perfect in nature. It was exactly what we needed for this to work.

I felt it and heard it, at the same time. All the dolphins chirped and pulsed out the signal to wake Mica. There was a blip in my head. For a second, I thought it had worked. Dragging him under the surface, I pushed and pulled, desperate to submerge my twin long enough to amplify the message through the water so it could get to him.

Then, light streamed into my brain and Mica squirmed in my arms. He dragged us both back to the surface, gasping for air as he burst above the water.

seventeen

THOUGHTS FLOODED MY brain as I hugged Mica, tight. Finally, after what felt like months, but was really only seconds, he hugged me back. Tears flowed down my face and into the ocean, like an offering to the gods. It was a drop in the bucket as far as ways to show appreciation went, but it wasn't something I could help.

"Cami, what the hell is going on here?" he asked, looking around. His sputtering stopped, and I saw the scene through his eyes: frothing seawater, black of night, a pod of over fifty dolphins making clapping sounds with their mouths.

Before I even got a chance to explain, Mica's dolphin took over. Though they had never met before, his dolphin beamed a bunch of images into Mica's brain, explaining everything. Because our twin link was back, I saw, too. He showed Mica sleeping, explaining in a way my dolphin hadn't, how the pod needed to wake him up, and why.

"So people have two hemispheres that work together, but dolphins actually have two brains?" he asked, sliding his hair from his eyes with his hand, like that could help him figure out what was going on in there. "What do I, I mean we, have then?"

"In our case, one side is human and the other one dolphin, as far as I can understand so far. So when the sonar shattered your cochlea ear, it short-circuited your brain, causing your body to think it was drowning. Your internal workings basically stopped to help you stay alive, as long as possible, underwater."

Mica looked at the water with fear in his eyes for the first time in his life. I hated that reaction, and tried to show him through images in my own brain that this was a good thing. I knew he'd figure it out eventually, but I also knew he was understandably scared. "I still don't understand," he said, hating the confusion he felt, treading water quickly, like he no longer trusted it to hold him safely. Now that I had him back, that made my heartache most of all.

"That can happen for lots of people who almost die from drowning, but don't. In our case, however, the magnetic burst of the sonar shifted the polarity in your brain, making the dolphin side more dominant."

"So I'm some sort of freak, is that what you're saying?" he said, and began to swim away with angry strokes.

I caught him quickly, in a way I'd never been able to even just a few weeks ago because he'd always been so much faster than me.

"It's not all that different from our clicks. The same thing that lets you hear me is what kept you alive all this time."

Mica looked back at the dolphins, still confused. But at least the anger was gone, for the moment.

"So if this is something we've had our whole lives, shouldn't Doc have figured this out?" he asked. The question was valid, and something I'd gone over with Billy and Celeste because it had confused me as well.

"He knows some of it, but not enough to really help. It goes back to the old legends about Dolphin Twins being a part of us. Turns out that genetically, it's true. They were so worried those traits would die out, they made sure we got some extra special versions of the strand of DNA that makes all of this real.

"All of our relatives, ancestors, have some of it, but we got an extra dose. So the actual separation of hemispheres is new for us, so no one could have predicted the way this played out." I noticed Mica shivering and felt bad. This was a lot to understand, especially when you've just woken up from a coma. I needed to get him out of the water. Even though I was reluctant to leave, I needed to get him home so my parents could see that this had worked, and so we could go get Shay and Andrew and wake them up too.

"No, I want to stay and hear, see, I don't know, what they have to say," Mica said, looking more like himself than he had a minute ago. I felt my dolphin's approval at this turn of events. She'd been worried that Mica's anger was targeted at them. But it was changing quickly to intrigue and hope.

"So how did The Elders do this with them?" he asked, biting his lip and looking for his particular dolphin, who came over and did a slow circle around us so Mica could look him in the eye.

I couldn't really explain it, but Mica's dolphin could. With slow images becoming clear, his dolphin showed us how Gram and everyone older than her had expected it, and their brain hemispheres came together slowly. Then he showed us how different the ocean was now. Years of drilling, of sonar, and recently, of fracking for oil, had set off a million little underwater explosions that led to a tiny tectonic plate-shifts underground. Now, the water and Island were more magnetic. The dolphins struggled with the way that felt every day. And now that I was in tune with them, I could tell that things literally didn't feel right.

It was like the difference between natural oil and an oil spill. The magnets underground were natural, useful, and good. But, when the ground cracked and too much of the magnetic forces were exposed; it led the whole world to shift.

Mica dipped his head underwater, like that would let him check up on everything the dolphin had shared. I laughed because that was such a Mica thing to do. "I'm so glad you're back," I said, squeezing him a bit harder than I should have.

"So my dolphin brain became dominant, responding to the trauma by slowing down, but why?" Mica asked, assimilating the information and adapting to communicating mentally with the dolphin at an alarming speed.

His dolphin answered back. When dolphins sleep, only half of their brain shuts down at a time. The two sides still linked together and communicated about everything— including waking the resting side from sleep. Humans sleep with their whole brain at one time. Mica didn't have another half of a dolphin brain to wake the sleeping side up.

"So I'd still be asleep if you didn't figure this out? Thanks Cami," he said, looking sheepish. I'd take the gratitude, considering he was awake now.

"They figured it out," I said, pointing to my dolphin and Mica's too.

"Yeah, but you figured out to listen to them. Good thing this didn't happen to you," he said, starting to shiver. I knew we'd have to leave the water soon.

I began to shrug but my dolphin flashed an image at me, which immediately went to Mica as well, from the night I had went down at the bonfire. My situation was a little different: my ear didn't exactly burst from a magnetic pulse from deep in the earth, but my head slamming on the rocks had a similar consequence. The extreme magnetic content on that part of the beach had shifted the polarity of my brain, too. But since my dolphin had been with me when it happened, she understood it immediately and woke me the moment I went down.

"But how? Why?" I asked, releasing Mica for long enough to kiss the silky rubber of her skin. She rubbed her melon to mine, pushing our foreheads together. She really was my guardian angel with fins for wings. She'd certainly proved she deserved a halo by now.

I still didn't understand why she'd been so tuned into my brain, just from us swimming together that short time. She made a series of sounds familiar to me—sounds I knew in my soul. The whistles and clicks from the ritual, during First Night had drawn her to me, and from that moment she'd been tuned in.

"Why did she come then, and not ever before?" Mica asked, getting all the info relayed.

She showed me how hard it had become to hear our chants, because we didn't know them well any more. Sometimes it worked, and the dolphins came, and sometimes it didn't. Part of the reason, was that everything that had been happening in the ocean caused cochlear damage on their end, too.

The damage wasn't instant, like with Mica and my friends, but more like a slow degradation from long-term exposure caused by extreme disturbances, underwater and underground. They couldn't hear us the same way they used to, with their ears. And our people had, for the most part, lost the ability to reach them with our minds and our hearts.

That night—when I felt more connected to nature, my past, my family, and my future—I'd reached her, and she'd given my brain a jolt of information that helped set me up for the fast recovery.

Thinking back, I'd felt the change instantly. But, I'd confused it with feelings for Blake. I woke up inexplicably drawn to him in that way that made me feel broken and put back together again. On the outside I looked the same, but I had changed on a molecular level, because of him and her.

The rest of the connection came quickly and my mental link with my dolphin had been improving steadily over the summer. The two sides of my brain were becoming increasingly proficient at working together. Every time I swam with my dolphin, my skills in her ocean-world multiplied exponentially. While the human part of my brain hadn't understood what she was saying, the dolphin part did, and it responded unconsciously, which is where all the ideas I didn't understand came from, like putting Mica in the water tonight.

"Ok, great—lucky you!" Mica said. His sarcasm was back. I had never been so grateful to hear his snarky side in my life. "If your brain was working so fabulously at piecing all of this together, why didn't you figure this out before? Shay's been down for over six weeks. Why couldn't they help her right away?"

I looked at him. Truly, I didn't know. But then, I understood. It was because it took me so long to believe.

If Blake and I had spent more time swimming with the dolphins together, instead of researching on computers, or fighting, or breaking into the lab, the mental link between us would have naturally increased as our dolphin brains connected.

The night he got hurt, Blake only passed out. His dolphin pulsed at him, attempting to shift his brain, but that wasn't what was required. Together, he and his dolphin understood enough to realize that, while it didn't work for him, it was exactly what the others needed.

But now, he was really, truly passed out from medical need. Both parts of his brain were in agreement that his body needed to be shut down to heal. It was a traditional coma. Unconscious, he couldn't use words to tell me what he knew, and we hadn't gotten to the place where we were linked with our minds.

My dolphin, Blake's dolphin and Blake had all sense what was going on, and they tried to tell me. I just didn't listen,   didn't believe. Not until Kaleb came back and showed me the crazy notions in my mind were true.

In addition to communicating with me, Kaleb had seen the details in Blake's brain, and was able to link the pieces together for all of us in a way the dolphins couldn't quite explain. I believed him about everything; because of the way he linked right into my brain.

"Oh my God! Kaleb," I said, looking off to the horizon to the place where I had left him last. Blake's dolphin cackled, and a picture that blurred the two of them appeared in my mind.

"What'd that little fucker do now?" Mica asked, gleefully floating in the water.

"He saved you," I said.

"Naw," Mica raised an eyebrow, dubious, and with good historical reason. But, that was the craziest part of it all.

"This all came together, because of him. He linked all the pieces because he was the only one who really believed."

Mica and I swam back under the protection of our dolphins, sharing the thrill of riding with them through the waves. His gratitude, his sheer glee at being back in the water—in addition to the joy of waking up and meeting his dolphin—kept us playing and swimming much longer than we planned. Distance needed to be covered in a hurry, in order to beat Mom and Dad for wake up; and my own sheer exhaustion was getting to me.

For the first time in a while, the swimming was hard for me. I'd been up for almost forty-eight hours, and time had truly stretched, making these two of the longest days of my life.

We arrived home, snuck into the house, and found both Kaleb and my father waiting up for us in Mica's room.

Kaleb, bless him, shared as much of the story as he was able, so when we arrived, my father was miraculously on our side. My mother was royally pissed, but it couldn't be helped. She tried to argue with me, but the proof was standing in his own room, dripping wet.

Desperate to see Blake and to rescue Shay and Darwen, Kaleb and I ran downstairs to catch Billy coming out of his house across the street, just as he was getting into his golfie. Blake, he'd just learned, was coming to. "Mica's awake. Take me with you and I'll fill you in," I demanded.

I wanted to be there when Blake woke up. I needed to apologize, to tell him I loved him and that he had been right. As we arrived in his room, he was barely stirring. Despite my not so peaceful protests, only Billy was allowed to stay. He closed the curtain and then, later, found Kaleb and I in the hall to give us an update.

"He's stable and coming out of the coma, which— unlike in the movies—may not happen right away. It's a slow process that could take most of the day, so you need to be prepared to wait."

I was prepared to wait forever. But I really wanted to get Shay in the water. I paced outside the room as Kaleb rolled his eyes, sensing how excited I was to see Blake.

Kaleb and I communicated silently, trying to use the time well. He was struggling to convince me that getting Shay in the ocean wasn't needed. He thought we could convince the two halves of her brain to flip back, or wake up, or do whatever the dolphins had done just by going into her room and explaining what to do.

I didn't think it was that simple. It was impossible to explain, considering he hadn't really been there, but merely telling the brain what to do wasn't enough. The suggestion was only part of it—the pulses, the energy generated by the dolphins and amplified by the water, the sacred swirl were required, too.

But, he was convinced he was right. So, instead of just waiting around for Blake to see us, we went into Shay's room to give it a try. Sadly, Kaleb's instinct had not been correct—which was why we were randomly shouting at Shay to wake up when Alysha found us.

"So, you put him in the water and the dolphins told him to wake up?" she asked, hope and confusion battling in her eyes.

"Basically, yeah," I said, glancing at Kaleb, seeking his silent opinion on exactly how much to say. It wasn't like I cared what he thought, per se, but I was torn. Just the fact that Mica was awake from swimming with dolphins seemed like a lot for everyone to take in.

"If it's so safe, and works so well, why are we hearing about this now?"

"Because Doc's a control freak with a hero complex, and our parents are stupid lemmings only capable of believing what they see," Kaleb said, cutting to the chase. "So, are you gonna help, or do we have to do this without you, too?"

Kaleb's words were harsh, but effective. Alysha agreed to wait until night. It was too risky, bordering on impossible, to get Shay and Darwen out in the day. Despite Mica's recovery, Alysha's and Andrew's parents didn't want their comatose children back in the water for any reason. We started plotting to do it anyway.

In the meantime, we waited for Blake to truly come-to. I'd seen him, hugged him, and held him. He'd said my name in a breathy voice, as he came in and out of consciousness while I'd kissed him and made the sacred swirl on his hand. All I really wanted to do was climb into bed with him, but considering the hospital and the way we'd left things, it wasn't exactly appropriate.

Instead, I covered every single part I could reach with kisses—his arms, his chest. I felt his eyes open again, and I heard him groan. Of course, Billy thought he was moaning from pain, and he banished me to the hallway. But, while I'd been with Blake, I'd had a flash of something, like I could hear him in my head, just the tiniest bit.

Mica's arrival was a source of huge celebration for the whole hospital. He was greeted by hollers and hugs. Doc, especially, looked surprised and insisted on examining him right away. While Mica was being looked over, I explained to my Mom, as best as I could, the details of what had happened. I begged for her forgiveness for going behind her back. When she gave it, I felt this was a tremendous meeting point for us; even though she didn't know about everything I'd done, I felt exonerated and forgiven, to the point I was actually ready to ask for permission to carry out the rest of our plan.

But then, Stoney walked in with Gramps. When they set eyes on Mica, well, pretty much all hell broke loose. They both laid into Doc and my mom for not coming up with the solution themselves.

I learned a lot in the blow out, namely that putting the injured in the water with the dolphins was hardly a new form of healing on the Island. For hundreds of years, the dolphins and our ancestors had worked together to provide healing for both.

When Doc's work became more complicated, he took over every aspect of medical needs on the Island. And then, his own baby, Helix's twin, had died in a dolphin-assisted birth, killing Doc's wife too. The reasons seemed unknown.

That's when Doc turned his back on the dolphins and closed the lab off to everyone else. When the new hospital opened, dolphin healing—at least in any kind of medically supervised fashion—was gone for good. The Elders continued to go to the water for aches and pains and small matters, but they kept it on the down-low. It was one more point of separation between them and the younger generation, who were reluctant to believe in anything they couldn't scientifically prove.

Weeks ago my grandfather had suggested putting the children into the water. He was turned down flat. Because of recent history—and specifically Doc's loss—he didn't push it.

After seeing Mica, and listening to the whole story, he ordered my mom and Doc to make it so. This was an order, not a suggestion, and it was exactly what Kaleb had wanted us to do. Again, he'd been right; we could have worked harder to get Gramps on our side.

The ambulances stirred the air with their sirens, and the sand with their wheels, as they brought Shay down to the shore. While Stoney was in favor of this solution, he was the Captain of The Guard. Tangible evidence of his cautious optimism was all around. What had been a private Hail Mary last night was a huge military operation now.

We'd waited until the last ferry left for the day, so they only had to clear a handful of locals off the beach between the old jetty and the pier. The beach was closed to everyone but Doc, some nurses, my mom, and the members of The Guard who were patrolling to keep possible onlookers away. They were staying put, they promised, though that had been a big debate. This was something that hadn't been done on-Island in twenty-odd years; since they'd lost one of the few babies born.

Gramps wanted a full ceremony, complete with all the Elders and drums. I think I'd broken his heart just a little when I told him we didn't need any of that to make it work. He insisted on joining us, and that I couldn't debate. Stoney came, too.

I felt like Alysha needed to be there, given what had happened last night, but she wasn't the swimmer her sister was. Luckily, Andrew was happy to hold her hand and help her feel confident in the ocean. The added safety of having Stoney present worked, as well.

Our location on the beach meant it was a shorter distance until we got out where we needed to be at sea. This second time we met with the dolphins, everything went much faster. We all knew what to do, and I was able to position Shay and Darwen in the center of the circle, while the rest of us worked to hold them up.

There were more dolphins in the bay this time, as even more of the pod showed up to help, knowing they were needed. We had an audience, and it included some non-believers.

I'd explained how important it was to be positive, while we waited for the ambulances to bring Shay and Darwen down to the beach. Words were unconvincing though, and I saw the concern in my friend's eyes. I understood why she was worried about getting in the water for this, but she needed to let it go.

And then, Mica showed up. His presence and his words worked in a way mine hadn't. For the millionth time that day, I was so, so, so glad he was there.

I left to call the dolphins closer to us, which was something only I could do.

When my girl arrived, she showed up with two more who looked familiar, but whom I really didn't know. Based on their interaction with Gramps and Stoney, it was obvious they knew them. I guessed they were Gramps' and Stoney's dolphins or, at least, Elders of the pod. We followed them out into the deeper part of the sea.

Again, the dolphins circled and started their calls. The extra energy from sheer numbers made it feel less like a pulse and more like an earthquake when we took Shay and Darwen underwater. The dolphins let their sonar go. The waves reverberated off the ocean floor, visibly moving the soot and some huge boulders, shifting things around. Something silver on the bottom caught my eye.

Before I could investigate, Shay and Darwen came to. Like Mica, they sputtered to the surface, to the surprise of everyone but the dolphins, and me. My girl winked, and blew water out of her blowhole in celebration.

While the others had a moment with Shay and Darwen, I took a minute to thank my girl. We were now—all of us—believers, again, in the link between our counterparts, the guardians in the sea, and ourselves.

Today, my dolphin had shown not just me, but all of us the way things needed to be. It was up to us to make sure that, collectively, we never forgot again. I promised her, over and over again, as we separated and swam our separate ways. She led her pod to the sea as I led mine to shore, so we could return to our various duties as The Guard for each other.

We got Shay and Darwen back to shore where it seemed most of the Island waited and cheered. They were overwhelmed, confused, and ecstatic. I knew how they felt.

There was so much to say and explain, but I was counting on Mica to handle it.

"You left me with Kaleb?" Blake asked. "Thanks a lot, Cami." My eyes went wide; worried he was still mad at me.

"We needed everyone else at the beach," I sputtered. "Be mad at me for not listening to you, for hurting you, but please don't be mad about this."

"Okay, love, I forgive you. For everything," he said, reaching for my hand and pulling me on the bed with his good arm.

I tripped onto him, every nerve in my body responding to being so close, but concerned I could hurt him stopped me from moving a single muscle. I desperately wanted to kiss him, but instead, I froze.

"You won't hurt me," he said, grinning, showing off the single dimple I hadn't seen in weeks.

"At least not like that," he said, silently broadcasting a fear of his own. Images of me with Kaleb flickered through my head, and I gasped. Not because of anything to do with Kaleb, but because I realized Blake's thoughts were clicking directly into my brain.

Concentrating, I looked at him, and thought carefully about how I spoke with Mica, Kaleb, and my dolphin, too.

With Blake, I saw even more. Hopes and fears came through, like he could hide nothing from me. I wondered if I sent the same to him.

If I shared my thoughts the way he was sharing his, he would be getting them unfiltered and unedited. He'd be reading me raw, getting everything from me. Would he know that I used to see him as a trap? That he had represented a life stuck on Pinhold, a limited future? I didn't feel like that anymore, but I didn't know if he would see the new feelings too.

"You and Kaleb clicked, didn't you?" he asked out loud. He did a good job, keeping the white heat of jealously from his voice, but he couldn't hide it in his brain. "I've been trying to keep his thoughts away, but it's like he's blasting them into my brain."

I gasped again, the depth of his feelings of betrayal coming through loud and clear. I was furious at Kaleb for using the connection he and I had shared as a weapon against Blake. The dimpled smile had turned to an angry pout as Blake stared into my eyes, like he was trying to pull the truth from me.

Worry and fear was etched into his face; jealousy burned from his eyes. Then, I felt that buzzing—those clicks inside my blood that didn't come from a single person or being, but from the universe when everything was lined up properly, and I'm in the right place doing the right thing at the right time.

Blake realized immediately what I meant to do seconds after I decided. His face lit up with a joy that blasted out the dark moodiness that had taken over again with just a few seconds of talk about Kaleb. No one else mattered at all, except he and I, alone in that room. And he got that from me; I made sure of it.

Remembering the way I'd shared all of the information with my dolphin, I leaned in and opened my mind, flooding him with my own point of view. I clicked everything, as raw and unfiltered as it could get, proving that head to heart, I was his and only his. He got it, and I got him.

Then kisses happened. Tons and tons of them. More than were really probably healthy in a hospital bed. But I didn't care. He was jealous of Kaleb, on a level I couldn't personally comprehend. But now that we shared clicks, I really saw for the first time how that felt swirling inside of him.

With every touch, I reminded him that I only did this with him. What we had together was singular, and his alone, way outside the scope of anything I'd ever shared with Kaleb. While Kaleb and I may have had a special connection, it felt nothing like this.

What Blake and I had now was ours alone. We'd flipped for each other on a subatomic level, attracted like magnets. This went beyond the physical, beyond the emotional and into cellular. Being with Blake had changed me for the better.

Because when you really click with someone, they become a part of you.

Forever.

about the author:

Amy Evans is a wife, mother, ocean lover and storyteller. She believes that all stories are better with kisses, and that wishes come true when they're shared. CLICKS is her first novel, nominated for best new release at the UtopYA conference for Young Adult and New Adult books. Five star reviews call it fresh, unique, fun.

To subscribe to news and updates via email:
http://amyevansbooks.com/newsletter

To order ECHOES, book two in the series:
http://amyevansbooks.com/ECHOESbn
http://amyevansbooks.com/ECHOESiB
http://amyevansbooks.com/ECHOESamz

To order PINK — a JELLYBEAN KISSES prequel:
http://www.goodreads.com/book/show/18629798-jellybean-kisses---pink---the-prequel

Connect with Amy:
www.facebook.com/amyevansclicks
www.twitter.com/aammyyss
www.amyevansbooks.com

READ ON FOR AN EXCERPT FROM ECHOES, BOOK 2!

CLICKS are moments of divine time, when the universe stops to tell you what's going to happen next. They're instincts, truths heard in your heart that are completely unique to you. (Book 1)

ECHOES are reverberations in the spiral of time, repeating lessons earlier generations never learned. They're louder and more dangerous than CLICKS, ideas that just won't leave you alone. They repeat over and over painfully til you listen, and cause damage if ignored. (Book 2)

ECHOES IS COMING SOON!

ECHOES

I STARED AT the water wondering how the glassy blue thirty-foot tubes of yesterday had turned into this huge mess of angry green foam ready to strip my flesh and spit out my bones. The waves were barely distinguishable and moved like thick mountains that looked impossible to pass. While I didn't plan to surf them, exactly, even paddling out was terrifying in conditions this perilous.

But this was one of the most important rescue-based events in the Surf Carnival, an extreme surf recuing competition. Since I was going for the most difficult certification in lifeguarding, we had to be prepared to rescue in any conditions. Surfers from all over the world came to experience the famous Pinhold waves, and they went out in the ocean, even when it was reckless, or closed.

So our island had a surf rescue team that helped when Beach Patrol couldn't. We called it The Guard, and it was our responsibility as a new generation to earn our place there and uphold the traditions of protecting the ocean and anything that went into them. It was more than just pride that prevented them from cancelling competitions. Any one accepted had to be prepared to perform rescues in every kind of circumstance. Today's ocean conditions came unexpectedly thanks to a hurricane on a faraway coast proving our oceans were all connected, even though it didn't look that way on maps.

Besides the whipping waves, all other signs pointed to a perfect Pinhold day of eighty degrees with clear skies and dolphins calling to one another off shore. My dolphin was out there. I could see flashes of her pale white skin. She watched from far past the break of the enormous waves, and shared what she could see with me via our sonar link.

From her perspective, we looked like little tiny, moving blobs that blended into the sand. I looked different than all the others through her eyes; brighter, with more detail, because I was familiar. And she was my dolphin twin.

Next to me stood Mica, my human twin, discussing conditions and circumstances with Gram as if I wasn't there.

"I don't think she should go," he said. The absolute conviction in his voice pissed me off.

"It's not your choice," my grandmother said. "This is Cami's competition, and if you get in The Guard, these are the exact conditions where you'll be called for rescue, so you need to know how to perform." She stood beside us on the beach, looking unimpressed as a cracked surfboard washed up by our feet.

I swallowed. Hard.

Most grandmas would scream and shout and do anything to keep their little ones from a scene as dangerous as this one. But not mine. A world-class elite athlete and former Olympian, she'd led Mica and me into similar situations as long as I could remember. She was a revered Elder on Pinhold Island, where we lived, charged with training the next generation, like Mica and me.

"Fear is a tool - let it sharpen you, make you stronger. You need to move forward. This is the way that I did it, and you can too," she said. Her words encouraged me. She and I had the same voice, along with the same body type and same long hair. Except that I still had the undercut the Alysha had done for me after my accident on First Night. The new growth was short but smooth, except where it was interrupted by a light, swirled scar. Genetically, Gram had given me everything I needed to succeed. And she'd trained with me almost every day even now in her sixties. I had no excuses to fail.

"I can do this," I muttered, trying to convince myself, as much as Mica and Gram, when I felt a strong hand touch my spine. Blake. His touches, even the innocent ones, were totally unique because of the way they radiated through me, every tingle echoed. He made it look so respectable, just a light hand on the center of my back. But even the tiniest stroke lit me up inside, distracting me from my nervousness, literally adding his strength and focus to mine.

"I know you can," he said. *For me, for Mica, for Shay,* he added telepathically. The added intimacy of communicating this way had my brain bursting with so much joy I had to close my eyes. We used the sonar we were born with to share silently, from mind to mind. We communicated like the dolphins did; every thought and feeling reverberated, strengthening the connection more each time.

I got in line with nine others, nodding my head at the ones I recognized. I adjusted my beanie - an unfortunate requirement I tolerated reluctantly, and shifted the weight of my heavy competition board. We weren't surfing today but paddling. So I hoisted the six foot monster onto my hips. As soon as the starter horn blasted, I took off from the shore.

I fought through the knee-high waves and tossed my body onto my board, using the forward motion to propel myself just a few feet. This event represented the life and death faced by surf rescue lifeguards, which I hoped to be, more than any other. I had to paddle my board out to sea to prove I could rescue even the most extreme surfers in the toughest conditions, and get them safely back to shore.

Already waterlogged, my board felt like home to me. But the usually friendly ocean did not. These waves weren't what I practiced in every day. The more I paddled, the more I realized all the elements seemed off. The water stung my skin and tasted irony, instead healing and sweet, the way it usually did. I had to fight against the waves for every inch, and I couldn't see more than three feet from my face with the constant, heavy sprays.

Popping from the water, I lost valuable time, but confirmed the placement of the first buoy in my path. The five hundred foot distance was a length I'd done easily even in my Nipper days, but right then, I battled for every single inch.

I duck-dove under the surface to make up some time, hoping that getting under the waves would get me away from the churn. I forgot to close my mouth, instantly regretting that lapse in judgment when I gulped sea water and my throat began to burn. I pushed forward, ignoring the pain, wondering if the water was hurting the dolphin I'd come to know and love that summer. I'd sensed her around before the race today, so maybe she'd ventured further out where the water, hopefully, wouldn't hurt her. Thinking of her should of been a distraction, but it wasn't.

Instead it connected me to all the swimming I'd done with her, even though the stroke I used today was very different. Dolphin swims were all trunk and tail, and board paddles were arms and kicks. But maybe I could combine the two. I still had no idea where anyone else was but I didn't worry about it. Instead I slipped towards the back of the board and wobbled. I was off balance, and the pressure of the water pushed me even further from the center. I re-calibrated my body and began to move my legs like they were one unit. I pushed the board with my core, feeling the water give way to a riptide moving under me.

I rode that and knocked into the second buoy, moving to the side before surfacing so I wouldn't get tripped around the bobbing target that I needed to pull off of the buoy to put on my board. At a thousand feet from shore, I couldn't see the beach at all. I felt all alone until I finally spied another competitor about twenty feet to the side of her buoy, so closer to mine. She'd gone twenty feet sideways and that would be hard to make up. I watched her try to maneuver her board sideways, and then refocused on myself.

I struggled to turn my now-weighted-down board back toward shore, gasping for air, pushing hard with my feet and arms. I missed getting purchase, and slid off the board and into the churning surf. A heavy wave came down, shooting me beneath the surface trapping me under six feet of fiberglass. And I panicked, worried about getting air.

Then I heard the clicks, calming beats from far away reminding me that I could do this, that I wasn't alone. Following her clicks and whistles, I slowed my heartbeat to match her rhythms and then I felt her; slippery skin and raw power under me. I stopped thinking and focused on her, and our connection didn't let me down. Instead she'd come exactly when I'd needed her, and literally lifted me up.

I chased oxygen, gasping for breath, as I grabbed back onto my rescue craft. The rocking waves made it practically impossible to stay no but she continued to help. Her muscled body stayed underneath, keeping the board steady as I got back into place. Securing the weight I needed to win and get my certification, I began to paddle, which was easier with her huge form propelling me.

I have to win this by myself. I clicked this to her, not knowing if she could understand the concepts of alone and win. Most dolphins lived in pods, and worked together for food and played together for fun. Helping each other was deeply ingrained from birth; their survival depended on it. In many ways, our survival depended on the same type of cooperation among The Guard members and the dolphins.

This land mammal / water mammal cooperation was a tenant our island life. But this contest included lifeguards from beaches up and down the coast, and I didn't want one of them to accuse me of cheating.

I had to go on alone. She nudged me forward into a particular swirl of current that pushed me right into the swell of a medium sized wave. I hit the sweet spot, sent her my gratitude, and rode it all the way in with some light paddling, which was all I could handle by that point. I could practically taste the win, could see the beach. If I could make it through the thundering crash, I would reach the finish line first. So I tucked my head, grabbed the weight and my board, and ran as hard as I could to the sand.

Made in the USA
San Bernardino, CA
23 April 2017